SPEAK WITH CONFECTION LARGE PRINT

AN AMISH CUPCAKE COZY MYSTERY BOOK 4

RUTH HARTZLER

Amish
ROMANCE BOOKS

I couldn't remember when I had last been so excited. I had closed on the new house I had bought from my twin sister, Rebecca, and her husband. They were Amish and I was not, but after my husband divorced me to marry a much younger woman, I had lived in the apartment over Rebecca's cupcake store with two elderly ladies, Eleanor and Matilda, and their cat, Mr. Crumbles.

Now Matilda, Eleanor, and Mr. Crumbles were moving into my new house with me, and I couldn't be happier. I was smiling widely to myself when Rebecca burst through the door of her store. "Sorry I'm late, Jane."

I looked at my watch. "You're not late. The shop doesn't close for another three hours."

Rebecca made a clicking sound with her tongue. "Of course I'm late. This is your first day in your new house, and I wanted you to have time off to enjoy it. It's just that I promised to help Mrs. Graber, and it took longer than I thought it would."

I waved her concerns away. "I work for you, Rebecca. I'm not going to shirk my duties just because I've bought a house. Besides, Eleanor and Matilda went to the house this morning. They said they'd get it ready for me." A small tingle of apprehension ran up my spine.

"Did you have many customers?"

I shook my head. "A steady stream, but I wasn't overwhelmed."

Rebecca pointed to the door. "Off you go!" Her tone was firm.

"But, but," I sputtered, but Rebecca would hear none of it.

She put her hands on her hips. "I insist!"

I didn't need telling twice. "*Denki*, Rebecca." I hurried out of the door and strode to my car. This was the first house I had ever owned —well, the first house I had owned all by myself, no cheating husband involved.

What's more, I wouldn't be lonely, not with Eleanor and Matilda. The house was far bigger than the apartment we had shared above the cupcake store, so I wouldn't be in for any surprises living with them. I hoped not anyway. Mr. Crumbles—he was another matter. That cat was full of surprises.

I brought the car to a stop and jumped out, smiling once more as I looked at my house. It was all white with a big porch and stood on the adjoining land to my sister and her husband's farm. They had been only too happy to sell it to me when their renters had given notice. That had coincided nicely with the arrival of money owed to me from my former marriage. The house was in good condition and solidly built, and what's more, it had electricity unlike other Amish-owned houses in the area. I was glad *Englischers* had rented it for years.

I looked over at the herb garden and the vegetable garden, and then all but skipped up the porch steps. I flung open the front door and gasped.

Eleanor and Matilda had decorated the house. It wasn't at all my style. I stood there with my mouth open, wondering where they had gotten all the furniture. Over to one side was a leather Chesterfield couch, but instead of being in the typical Chesterfield colors of brown or black, this one sported the brightest floral pattern I had ever seen. I almost needed sunglasses to look at it.

Opposite it was a huge wooden table with a slab of marble on the top.

A huge chandelier hung from the ceiling. It looked antique. I was certain it hadn't been there before. Bright purple curtains hung from the windows opposite me. I wondered whether Eleanor and Matilda were both color-blind. That was when I turned around and saw what was on the far wall.

I couldn't believe my eyes. Swords and daggers and guns covered the wall, collectively forming some bizarre type of decoration. They hadn't been in the apartment—not as far as I knew—and I wondered where they had been hiding them.

Matilda walked into the room. She let out a scream when she saw me. "Eleanor, she's here!" she yelled. To me, she said, "You're early." Her tone was accusatory.

I rubbed my temples. "Yes, I know you wanted to surprise me, but..." My voice trailed away.

"Well, you *have* surprised us," Matilda said.

It was then I noticed she was covered in soapsuds. I heard a sound like someone being strangled. "Is there somebody else here?" I asked her.

Matilda looked aghast. "Somebody else here? Have you taken leave of your senses, Jane?"

"Very probably," I admitted. I hurried over to her, but she barred the doorway. After some jostling with elbows, I managed to push past her. The noise was coming from the main bathroom.

I flung open the bathroom door to see Eleanor sitting in the bath with a goat.

I thought perhaps I was having a nightmare, a rather bad nightmare. Surely, this couldn't be happening. "Eleanor, why are you in the bath with a goat?"

"I didn't do it deliberately," she said rather crossly. "I was giving the goat a bath. She resisted, and I fell in."

The goat let out another mournful sound.

I took a deep breath. "Why on earth are you shampooing that goat? And isn't it one of those wild goats?"

"Gigi *was* a wild goat, but we are training her, aren't we, Matilda?"

Matilda nodded enthusiastically. "She's the tamest of the wild goats."

Some time ago, Matilda and Eleanor had rescued fifteen wild goats for a petting zoo at a fundraising event and had subsequently boarded them on my sister's farm. The wild goats had caused no end of trouble, and my sister and her husband were thrilled when I said the goats could live with me. After all, the house came with several acres.

"Why are you washing the goat, anyway? And more to the point, why are you washing a goat in my bathtub?"

"Where else would we wash her?" Eleanor frowned so hard, her eyebrows met and formed a unibrow. "Don't worry, we didn't use your shampoo and conditioner. We bought some specially." She pointed to the bottle at the foot of the bath.

I tiptoed across the soaked bathroom floor and picked it up. The label proudly announced, 'Premium Shampoo for Goats.' I was shocked. "They actually make shampoo for goats? Who in their right mind shampoos goats?"

Eleanor appeared quite offended. "We entered Gigi in the goat show."

Well, now I had heard everything! I folded my arms over my chest. "You can't put that goat in a show! Goats need pedigrees and everything like that. People breed them carefully for years. You can't put any old goat in a goat show."

"They introduced a new class this year," Matilda said from behind me.

I turned around halfway so I could keep an eye on both her and the goat. I didn't want any more surprises.

She pushed on. "The class is called *Any Other Variety*. They did it to allow anybody to enter any type of goat, because the goat society was trying to get the general public interested in showing goats."

Eleanor nodded, causing bits of soapsuds to fly from her hair. "And what a good idea it is too. Matilda, could you hand me that blue rinse?"

Matilda handed Eleanor a bottle of blue liquid, and she wasted no time pouring it over the goat. I expected the goat to object, but now she seemed to be enjoying the attention.

At that point, I was very pleased that the house had an en-suite bathroom and that the goat was being washed in the main bathroom. "About all the furniture," I began.

Matilda interrupted me. "We had it in storage for so many years and now it can see the light of day. Isn't it wonderful!"

"That's one word for it," I said. "And what about all the guns on the wall?"

"They don't work," Matilda said cheerfully. "They're only for show. But don't worry. The katanas and daggers can certainly be used as weapons. They make a lovely and useful display too, don't they?"

I clutched my head with both hands. I was beginning to regret buying the house and wanted to go back to the apartment. I staggered out of the bathroom and headed for the kitchen. I needed to make myself a nice cup of hot meadow tea. I had been raised Amish and left the community after my *rumspringa*. Some of the Amish ways had stuck with me, such as considering hot meadow tea to be soothing.

I found Mr. Crumbles sitting under the kitchen table. "I think I should get under there with you."

Matilda walked into the kitchen. "Jane, you're worrying about nothing." She shook her head and frowned. "It must be the excitement of seeing how beautifully we decorated your house, and the shock of owning your own home and all these lovely acres filled with our goats. And don't worry about us taking the goat to the show. It's only a goat show. What could go wrong?"

2

When we arrived at the goat show, I sat in the car, my hands trembling. I had no idea Matilda and Eleanor intended to transport Gigi in my car. I had expected they would hire a goat or livestock transport company. The goat had tried to escape from my car the entire way to the goat show, which had made driving difficult. I'd had to drive slowly to be safe, despite Matilda and Eleanor loudly and insistently urging me on.

As it was, we had arrived at the goat show plenty early. I took a deep breath and watched as Matilda and Eleanor did their best to encourage the goat to walk into the exhibition building. Just as they had almost reached the entrance, a well-dressed woman walked in front of them. She waved her arms. Even from the distance, I could tell she was angry.

Matilda managed to get the goat to walk around the woman, even though the woman kept trying to jump in front of Gigi.

I jumped out of the car and ran to their assistance, but the woman left.

"What was that incident with that woman?" I asked them.

"It was some stuck-up, irate woman who said we shouldn't bring a goat like that to the show," Eleanor said. "I told her Gigi was entered in the Any Other Variety class, but that didn't make her any happier."

"Don't let that worry you now," Matilda said. "Have positive thoughts. What that woman said was simply her own opinion."

Eleanor nodded and maneuvered Gigi inside. Goats were everywhere: white goats, multi-colored goats, chocolate colored goats with white markings, and black goats with white markings. None of them looked anything like Matilda and Eleanor's wild goat, but then again I hadn't expected that they would.

I looked up to see Eleanor and Matilda struggling with Gigi. Other goat owners were looking on, their jaws gaping open.

Finally, they managed to get Gigi into a pen. The other goats were all standing politely in their individual pens while their owners fussed over them and groomed them. Eleanor and Matilda were hanging tightly onto Gigi.

I walked over to them. "Gigi doesn't look anything like the other goats," I said in the most even tone I could muster. At least the smell was pleasant—the combined fragrance of hay and heavily scented shampoo permeated the air.

Eleanor's eyebrow shot skyward. "Of course not. She's in the Any Other Variety class. We told you that."

The lady in the next pen apparently overheard because she leaned over to us. "This is a dairy goat show," she said with a chuckle.

Eleanor nodded to Gigi. "Isn't this a dairy goat?"

The woman chuckled again. "No, definitely not. She's a crossbred goat, probably a combination of fleece and meat goats."

"Someone wouldn't eat Gigi, surely?" Eleanor said in alarm.

"I'm Francis." The woman stuck out her hand.

"That's a pretty goat you have there," I said, shaking her hand.

Francis beamed from ear to ear. "Yes, her name is Splendiferous Farms Lady Prudence. She's in the junior goat class."

I stared at the goat. "What type of goat is she?"

"She's a Toggenburg. They're the brown ones with white markings." Francis gestured to pens beside her filled with large and substantial-looking goats. "Next to these Toggenburgs are Alpines, and in the pens beyond are Saanens. They're the white ones."

"What breed are those multi-colored ones with droopy ears?" I asked her.

"Nubians. And over the back are the LaManchas, the Oberhaslis, and the Dwarf Goats."

Something puzzled me. "Why is there an Any Other Variety class at this show? I mean,

Matilda and Eleanor told me it was to encourage people to become interested in goat showing, but wouldn't it be an Any Other Variety class for dairy goat breeds only?"

Francis shook her head. "There *is* no other variety of dairy goat outside the classes here. The Any Other Variety class was introduced so farmers could bring maybe an Angora goat or a Cashmere goat. It's not a recognized, serious class, of course. I don't think it was meant for crossbred goats, although your goat is obviously full of character," she added kindly, although I'm sure that wasn't what she really thought. "Have you had your goat for long?"

Matilda shook her head. "We're still trying to teach her to lead."

Francis was visibly disturbed. "Oh, that's not good. The judges expect them to lead very well. All the show goats are very well behaved, just like dogs at a dog show. They all have to walk around politely and then stand for the judge."

Matilda and Eleanor exchanged glances. "You don't have to enter Gigi in the show. We can always go home," I said hopefully.

Eleanor was visibly put out. "We're not going home. Besides, I haven't seen any other goats that look like Gigi, so maybe she's the only entrant. That means we'll get first prize."

"That's cheating!" Matilda exclaimed.

Eleanor's face flushed beet red. "How is it cheating, Matilda?"

Thankfully, Francis interrupted them. "I did see some Cashmere goats on my way in. Never mind—don't expect to win at your first show."

"Do you think *you* will win?" Matilda asked her.

"I certainly hope Prudence will win her class. She was Reserve Champion Toggenburg at her last show, which was bigger than this show. The only thing is, Gemma Calhoun's goat, Liberty Hill Farm Sweetened Wine, always wins Grand Champion."

"Does she win Champion Toggenburg goat or champion of all the goats?" I asked her.

"Both," she said with a sigh. "She always wins her class and then goes on to win Best of Breed, and then she always wins Best in Show as well. In fact, her goat has never been beaten." She cast a look around her. "I saw Gemma's trailer outside, but I haven't seen her." She lowered her voice and added, "She's not a very nice person. None of the other breeders like her."

I scratched my forehead. "I didn't see any trailers when we arrived."

"You must've parked out the front. All the trailers are out the back. How did you get that goat here?"

"In my car," I said with a glare at Matilda and Eleanor. They both looked away.

"Well then, I had better get Prudence to her class." She sprayed something all over the goat, which made her coat shine, and then led her out of the pen.

"Maybe we should have bought some of that stuff." Matilda leaned over the pen and looked at it. "It's some sort of spray-on shine for show horses."

"I don't think it will help Gigi," I said. Both of them glared at me, so I thought it was time to walk away. I walked over to the ring and sat down to watch the entrants. All the goats looked the same to me, but I expect it was like show dogs—there were particulars that only breeders and exhibitors would recognize.

The goats walked around the ring one after the other. I was rather dismayed when I saw how well behaved they all were. Presently, the exhibitors lined up in the center of the ring and the judge walked along, inspecting each goat. The goats were awarded ribbons and left the ring.

Next, it was Francis's turn. All the goats seem to be as shiny as each other. I noticed Francis was looking straight at the judge, maybe expecting the judge to call her goat in first. In fact, that was what happened. This time, the judge took longer to look at the second and third goats, but soon, the ribbons were awarded and Francis's goat won.

Then came the announcement I had been dreading. "And now the Any Other Variety Goat, any age," came the blaring announcement over the loudspeaker.

I sank back into my seat, trying to make myself look inconspicuous. Some beautifully groomed goats walked in—I assumed they were the Cashmere goats Francis had mentioned, as they had long woolly hair. They too behaved as perfectly as the other goats had. There were some taller goats, but I had no idea what breed they were. Then came Eleanor, half leading, half dragging Gigi. She managed to get Gigi into the ring and behind the others to join the circle. I noticed the exhibitor directly behind her walked out of the regular line, giving Gigi a wide berth.

The judge this time was a man. I couldn't see his expression when Gigi arrived, but I could only imagine.

All the goats walked around politely, all except Gigi who pulled back and then did a couple of jumps forward. Still, it was all going better than I thought. I hadn't expected that Eleanor would be able to get her to walk on the leash at all.

I jumped when a voice spoke beside me. I turned to see Matilda. She was rubbing her hands with glee. "They're doing awfully well, aren't they!"

"Um, err, yes," I lied.

The judge indicated they should all line up. He indicated Gigi should line up last. Gigi did not want to stand still. She ran around Eleanor in circles, wrapping the leash around her legs. Eleanor fell down face forward and the goat stood on her back.

"Shouldn't we help her?" I leaped to my feet, but Matilda pulled me back down. I landed on the hard wooden seat with a thump.

"No! She'll be disqualified and won't win anything if you help her. That's what happens with Olympic marathon runners. Assistance means disqualification."

"But this is a goat show, not an Olympic marathon," I protested.

Matilda shook her head and glared at me. "No! I'm sorry, you will have to leave her alone. She won't win if you help her."

"She's not going to win anyway," I said. "She's in last place, and all those other goats are well-behaved." *And much better looking*, I added silently.

When I looked back up, I saw that Eleanor had miraculously gotten herself out of the mess. She was now standing once more and was clutching Gigi around the neck. The judge had now reached her. He bent down to take a closer look.

"This isn't good," Matilda muttered.

"What do you mean?"

"Didn't you notice? The judge asked the other exhibitors to show him their goats' mouths. We didn't practice opening Gigi's mouth."

I didn't know what to say. I watched as Eleanor placed her hands in Gigi's mouth, encouraging her to open her mouth for the judge. "Why does the judge want to look in the goats' mouths?"

"I expect he wants to see their teeth or something," Matilda said.

The judge bent down, his long white beard approaching Gigi's face.

Suddenly, Gigi jumped forward. She grabbed his beard in her teeth. I don't know if the judge got a good look at her teeth, but I'm sure all the spectators did. She chewed on his beard while the judge screamed and flailed his arms.

I jumped to my feet, intending to go to the judge's assistance, when an unaccompanied Toggenburg goat ran into the ring.

A spectator behind me gasped. "That's Liberty Hill Farm Sweetened Wine!"

I heard a high-pitched scream. A woman ran into the ring and turned to face the crowd. "She's dead! Gemma Calhoun is dead!"

3

The next few minutes were a blur. People ran around in a panic, and the sound of screams cut through the air. Eleanor somehow made Gigi release the judge's beard, and she managed to wrestle her back to her pen. "What happened?"

I clutched my throat. "You know as much as I do. Somebody yelled that Gemma Calhoun was dead."

Francis appeared at our side. "It was murder!" Her voice trembled.

"Are you sure?" I asked her.

She nodded. "I had been to the bathroom, and then I was buying some coffee when one of the stewards I knew told me Gemma had been murdered. He said nobody can leave the grounds because the police are on their way."

Before she could say any more, the loudspeaker sputtered. "Ladies and gentlemen, there has been an unfortunate incident. The police have asked everybody to remain in place until they can question you all. Nobody is allowed to leave." The microphone crackled and then cut out.

"But I didn't hear a shot," Francis protested.

Matilda stepped forward. "Maybe the murderer used a silencer. Or maybe the vic was stabbed or garroted."

Eleanor piped up. "Or simply strangled. Or maybe she was hit over the head with a blunt object, or maybe she was poisoned. There are many types of poison that can kill quickly."

"Honestly, Eleanor, we don't know if the vic was poisoned," Matilda said in a scolding tone. "And if she was, then we don't know that the poison was administered recently. Maybe it had been building up over time." She turned to Francis. "Did the vic appear healthy? Was her hair falling out?"

Francis's face grew paler.

"We don't know the method of murder," I said to Matilda and Eleanor. "I think it's time to change the subject. Francis isn't looking too well."

Francis sat down on a wooden stool. "I'm all right. I feel terrible that I said nobody liked Gemma, and now she's dead."

"You were simply telling the truth," Matilda said. "Obviously, *somebody* didn't like her, or she would still be alive." Matilda ignored my warning glance and pushed on. "And Jane, maybe your detective will show up."

I rubbed my hand over my forehead. "He's not *my* detective."

I had not seen Detective Damon McCloud for some time as he had been called away to give evidence on a case. I had no idea if he was back in town yet. While we were not yet dating, I was certain our relationship was progressing in that direction. I was thinking this over when Matilda elbowed me hard in the ribs. "Isn't that him over there?"

I looked up but only saw the back of a man's head disappearing through a door. However, I did recognize the other man, Detective Carter Stirling, a rather unpleasant man with an attitude. "It could be Damon, but I only saw the back of his head."

"It was him," Matilda said. "I'm certain of it. My observation skills are second to none."

"The police are going to interview us all!" Francis's voice rose to a high pitch. "That means they think one of us did it."

"But one of us *did* do it," Matilda said. "The victim died, I assume, in this very building."

"But maybe the poison was administered to her some time ago," Eleanor pointed out.

"As I already told you, Eleanor, we don't know if it *was* poison yet," Matilda said. "As usual, you're jumping to conclusions. And maybe you should feed Gigi some more hay so she doesn't climb out of her stall."

I shot a look at the goat. Indeed, she had finished the hay and was sizing up the wall of the pen.

Instead of protesting, Eleanor threw some hay in with her. "I don't think showing a goat was such a good idea," she admitted. "Maybe we should show Mr. Crumbles instead."

"I'm sure they don't have any classes for Any Other Variety at cat shows," I said firmly.

Eleanor waved one hand at me in dismissal. "Oh, it's perfectly all right, Jane. You don't lead a cat around on a leash at a cat show. You simply put them in a cage."

"I don't think Mr. Crumbles would take too kindly to a cage."

Eleanor nodded slowly. "Yes, I do think you're right."

"You again!"

I spun around to see Detective Stirling standing there, his hands on his hips.

"Do you three have to get involved with *every* murder in this town?"

Francis gasped.

"We were simply showing our goat," I said, my tone angry.

Detective Stirling took one step forward. "Be that as it may, nobody is allowed to leave until we take everybody's statements."

"Was she shot?" Matilda asked.

The detective looked somewhat taken aback. "Excuse me?"

Matilda cupped her hand to his ear and said loudly, "Was she shot?"

Detective Stirling bristled. "I heard you the first time. You can't ask me that question. It's an ongoing investigation."

Matilda shook her head. "You haven't taken my point. My point is that if the vic was shot or stabbed, then everybody here could be a suspect, but if she was poisoned with a slow-acting poison, then it possibly wouldn't be anyone here at all."

A slow red flush traveled up Stirling's face. He opened his mouth, but before he could say anything, Damon appeared at his elbow. "Hello Jane," he began sheepishly, but Stirling cut him off.

"We need to have a word." He jerked his head to a row of seats over by the wall and the two walked over.

"I wonder what that's all about?" I said.

I didn't have long to wait because they came back presently. "I won't be on this case," Damon said. "Detective Stirling will be interviewing everybody."

With a curt nod, Stirling addressed Francis. "And you are?"

"Francis Smith."

"And what are you doing here?"

"I'm showing my goat, of course." She pointed to her goat.

Stirling peered at the goat. "And is that goat in direct opposition to the victim's goat?"

"Well, um, well, yes," Francis stammered. She was quick to add, "But all the goats here are. It's a competition, a goat show."

Damon tapped me under the elbow and led me away a few paces. "I was going to call you. I only got back into town late last night and then got called here on this case. Anyway, it looks as though I'm off the case."

"I don't understand," I said. "Why would they call you out on the case and then..." My voice trailed away.

Damon's ears turned pink and he shuffled from one foot to the other. "Um, Carter, that is, Detective Stirling, um thinks I might be prejudiced on your behalf, and you're a suspect—in his eyes at least," he finished lamely.

I rubbed my forehead and sighed. "I see. Damon, was she shot?"

He cast a look over at Detective Stirling. "No, she was poisoned, but keep that to yourself."

"Surely we're not suspects? We had never even met the woman. Matilda and Eleanor simply wanted to show their goat. In fact, we had never even heard of the victim until

Francis, the lady over there, told us that she always wins."

"Look, I'm sure Carter will sort that all out," Damon said. "I wouldn't worry about it too much, Jane. He'll just take your witness statements and then you'll be able to go. I doubt you'll hear from him again. After all, as you say, none of you had a motive, and you hadn't even met the victim."

"I'm sure you're right." Still, the sinking feeling in the pit of my stomach wouldn't go away. Detective Stirling was now talking to Matilda and Eleanor, and they looked none too pleased. I couldn't hear what he was saying to them.

I was worried why Damon hadn't called me. Maybe he didn't have the same feelings for me any longer. Or maybe I had imagined his feelings in the first place. His next words put me at ease. "Jane, maybe I could call you soon and we could have dinner?"

I tried not to look too pleased, but I could feel my face burning. I was certain I was blushing. "That would be lovely," I said in the most even tone I could muster.

Damon smiled from ear to ear. "Then I had better get going before Carter gives me a hard time. I'll be in touch." With that, he tapped me briefly on the arm and disappeared.

Matilda and Eleanor hurried over to me. "Detective Stirling is a fool," Eleanor said.

I expected Matilda to rebuke her, but she readily agreed. "He certainly is! Do you know what he said to us, Jane?"

"No," I began, but she interrupted me.

"He said it was a well-known fact that Gemma Calhoun was vehemently opposed to the Other Variety Class at the show and he thinks that gave us a motive for murder."

"But there's no prize money, just a ribbon, and besides, you didn't have a hope of winning!"

Both of them appeared quite offended. "Maybe Gigi would have won if she hadn't eaten the judge's beard," Eleanor protested. "Detective Stirling said people enter these shows for the glory, and he said we're all suspects. Jane, we don't want the police to look too closely at us."

I was puzzled. "What do you mean?"

Matilda cleared her throat and glared at Eleanor. "She means we don't want to be suspects. Jane, we have to solve this murder, and the sooner the better."

4

As soon as I walked into my sister's house, I relaxed. I remembered my Amish childhood as being a peaceful one, despite the fact I had worked hard. I didn't remember the stresses and strains of everyday life I now experienced as a non-Amish person, and I didn't think that was simply because I had been looking through the rose-tinted glasses of childhood.

"*Wilkom*," Rebecca said. "Come in, all of you." She cast a look at our feet. "Your cat isn't with you?"

"No, we thought it would be rude to bring him with us," Eleanor said.

Rebecca was visibly relieved. "Then come in. Ephraim is stoking the fire."

We walked into the plain living room. Ephraim straightened up when he saw us. "The nights are starting to cool a little already," he said, to a murmur of agreement.

"I believe you took one of the goats to a show today?" His lips twitched at the sides.

"Yes, and somebody was murdered," Matilda announced.

Rebecca shot me a sharp look. "You didn't tell me that, Jane!"

"I didn't want to worry you."

"Worry me? Why do you always think I'll be worried?

Matilda appeared oblivious to the tension and pushed on. "Yes, she was apparently a famous goat breeder. Jane said she was poisoned."

I put my finger to my lips. "Hush, Matilda. Damon asked me not to tell anybody. I told you that in confidence."

Rebecca's eyes shot skyward. "Damon? The nice detective?"

I sighed long and hard. Maybe this dinner wasn't going to be quite so peaceful, after all.

Rebecca ushered us to the table. After everyone took their places, I went with her to the kitchen to help.

"Didn't you say you hadn't heard from the detective for a while?"

I nodded. "Yes, apparently he got back to town last night."

Rebecca frowned. "And he hadn't contacted you in all that time?"

"No, but he did invite me to have dinner with him."

Rebecca clasped her hands in delight. "*Wunderbar*! Now help me carry this to the table."

We carried bowls of mashed potato, chicken gravy, bread, butter, a pot of brewed coffee, and salted pretzels to have with the ice cream for dessert. In this community, desserts that wouldn't melt during the first course were always put out on the dinner table at the same time as the main meal.

I took my seat, and we all closed our eyes for the silent prayer which the Amish had before every meal, and in this community, after every meal as well. I always knew when to open my eyes. I had long ago given Matilda and Eleanor the tip to say the Lord's Prayer and then open their eyes when they finished it. On this occasion, they must have recited the Lord's Prayer rather quickly because when I opened my eyes, theirs were already open. When they saw me looking at them, they both shut their eyes. I resisted the urge to laugh with some difficulty.

"Do you like your new house?" Ephraim asked me.

"It's wonderful. I'm so glad you sold it to me."

"It will be *gut* having you living so close," Rebecca said.

Matilda quirked one eyebrow. "But she was close to you when we were living in the apartment over your cupcake store. You probably spend more time there than you spend here."

Rebecca chuckled. "Well, it's the thought that counts."

I ate some mashed potato and then looked up to see Matilda and Eleanor eating their food hungrily. "This is good," Matilda said when she had finished her mouthful. "What do you call this?"

"It's pot pie," Rebecca said.

"It doesn't look like a pie."

"It's probably called pot pie after *bot boi*, which is the Pennsylvania Dutch name for square noodles," I explained. "I expect *Englischers* heard the name and thought it was *pot pie,* but it's more like chicken and dumplings—you know, square noodles with chicken and gravy, and vegetables, sometimes only potatoes. I've made it for you. Don't you remember? I laid the strips of pastry out to dry on the back of a kitchen chair."

"Ah yes, but you haven't made it for a while though, Jane." Matilda shot me a reproachful look. "And I don't think you ever said the name of it, but yes, it is rather delicious."

"So what news do you have of the community?" I asked Rebecca.

"Oh, it's the same as usual," she said. "The bishop and his wife are well. Our children are *gut*. Everyone is *gut*."

"And I see that your goats haven't escaped," Ephraim said with obvious relief.

"Thanks to you raising the fence," I told him. "I had no idea goats could jump so high."

"*Jah*, goats can jump quite high from a standstill and wild goats even more so," he said. "I'm sure that fence will keep them in, and there are those old tree stumps in the center of the field that the goats can stand on."

"It's ideal for goats," Eleanor said. "They do enjoy standing on things."

"And they enjoy eating beards," I told them. "Did they ever try to eat your beard, Ephraim?"

Ephraim dropped his fork. "Eat my *baart*? *Nee*, but I didn't get close enough to them. What do you mean?"

I told them the whole story of how Gigi had devoured the judge's beard. Rebecca and

Ephraim doubled over with laughter. They were still laughing when there was a knock on the door.

Amish people often visited each other at mealtimes, but still, an uneasy feeling settled in the pit of my stomach. Ephraim crossed to the door and opened it. My heart sank when I heard Detective Stirling's voice.

The detective strode in scant moments later, followed by a uniformed police officer. "There is a discrepancy in your stories," Stirling snapped.

"My, my story?" I stammered.

"No, *their* stories." He jabbed his index finger in the direction of Matilda and Eleanor.

Both jumped to their feet. "What nonsense!" they said in unison.

"You said you had never met the victim."

"But we hadn't," Matilda protested.

"I have witnesses who stated that the three of you exchanged words as you were leading your goat to the entrance of the exhibition building."

Matilda and Eleanor exchanged glances. "A woman did tell us we had no business having our goat there, but she didn't give her name, and we had never seen her before," Matilda said.

Stirling was unmoved by their protests. "You have to come down to the station and give your statements. Come with me now." He turned to me. "And you, Miss Delight, we are impounding your car."

I was aghast. "My car! Why?"

"We need to examine it for evidence of a possible crime. It will be returned to you in due course."

I grabbed Matilda's arm as she made to go past me. "Should I call you a lawyer?"

Matilda patted my hand. "No, leave it to us." She and Eleanor walked to the door with the detective and the uniformed officer behind them.

"I asked them to leave their guns outside," Ephraim said after they'd left.

"Never mind that," Rebecca said. "Jane, you had better explain what's going on."

"I must admit I'm at a loss." I threw my hands to the ceiling. "When we arrived at the goat show, a woman yelled at Matilda and Eleanor. I couldn't hear what she said because I was in the car, but she waved her arms and looked quite annoyed. They told me she said they had no business taking a wild goat to a goat show. Now, it seems she was the murder victim today."

Rebecca shook her head. "But why did they take your car?"

I shrugged. "The victim was poisoned. Maybe the detective will look for traces of poison in my car. I don't have a clue, to be honest."

Ephraim drew the back of his hand across his brow. "Surely the detective wouldn't think that two elderly ladies murdered someone because she insulted their goat."

"I have no idea, to be honest," I told him. "Another lady at the goat show said nobody liked the victim. Her name was Gemma Calhoun. Apparently, she was quite unpopular. We were told that her goat always won everything. Maybe another competitor murdered her."

"People must take those goat shows quite seriously," Ephraim said.

I shrugged. "Who knows? Maybe she was very wealthy and her heir murdered her. Or maybe she was having an affair and the man's wife killed her out of jealousy. Or maybe..."

Rebecca interrupted me. "Jane, you're beginning to sound like Matilda and Eleanor."

"Oh." I knew she didn't mean it as a compliment. "I hope they're all right. Detective Stirling is quite intimidating."

"Matilda and Eleanor didn't appear intimidated in the least," Ephraim said.

I had to admit he was right. "I wish there was something I could do. You heard Matilda—she said I couldn't get them a lawyer. I just wish there was something I could do," I said again.

"You could pray, of course," Ephraim said.

"And you could eat the rest of your dinner," Rebecca added. "You won't be of any use to anybody if you starve yourself."

I patted my stomach. "I've cleaned up my plate already. I hardly think I'm in danger of starving."

"Then have some ice cream with pretzels. You need to keep up your strength."

I was puzzled. "My strength? What for?"

"To solve the case, of course," Rebecca said. "It's clear Detective Stirling suspects Matilda and Eleanor. And without your detective on the case, somebody has to prove him wrong." She hesitated and then added, "Why isn't Detective McCloud investigating the case?"

"Detective Stirling suggested he shouldn't because of me," I said, my cheeks burning.

Ephraim and Rebecca exchanged glances and then both nodded slowly.

I could scarcely eat the ice cream with the salted pretzels despite the fact it was normally one of my favorite foods. After we finished, Rebecca insisted I eat some chocolate whoopie pie cupcakes and drink some meadow tea, but my stomach was churning.

I jumped when my cell phone pinged. I looked down to see a message from Matilda.

Everything's fine. Will tell you

about it tonight. Please
thank Rebecca and
Ephraim for us. We'll go
straight home.

I read the message to Rebecca and Ephraim.

"See, there was no cause for concern," Rebecca said.

I nodded and kept my opinion to myself. I was agitated during the short walk to my house. It was night, but there was a half moon and a strong breeze, and the shadows of branches flittering over the pathway in front of me made me jumpy. I wondered how Matilda and Eleanor would get back, but I figured that since the police had collected them, the police would take them home.

I unlocked the door, flung it open, and gasped.

5

The wall, where once hung guns, daggers and swords, was bare. Had we been robbed? My blood ran cold.

I gasped again as someone appeared in the doorway. "Matilda!" I shrieked.

"Were you expecting somebody else?" She was clearly perplexed.

I pointed to the wall. "It's all gone! Everything! The guns, the swords!"

Eleanor appeared at her side. "Of course. Since we're suspects in the murder case, it wouldn't do for us to have weapons hanging on the wall."

"You said the guns were just for show."

Matilda and Eleanor exchanged glances. "Still, we can't take any chances," Matilda said. "We've just made ourselves some coffee. Eleanor, go fetch it. Jane, would you like some?"

I looked at my watch. "What, coffee? At this time of night?"

"We're going to need coffee because we have some work ahead of us," Matilda said.

Eleanor returned with the coffeepot and three cups. "Let's get to work."

I was almost afraid to ask. Instead, I asked, "Was the questioning rough?"

"We've had worse," Matilda said with a shrug of one shoulder. "Still, it's clear that Stirling sees us as suspects."

"Just because you had words with the victim?"

Eleanor nodded. "He seems to be clutching at straws, so we need to find out who committed the murder and fast."

Two laptops were already on the coffee table. Mr. Crumbles was sitting on one of them.

"Mr. Crumbles is upset." Eleanor picked him up and clutched him to her. "He knows something is wrong."

Mr. Crumbles' expression remained unchanged. I doubted he thought anything was wrong, but I didn't comment. "What do we do?"

"You fetch your laptop, Jane. We will all search Gemma Calhoun and see what we can come up with."

Eleanor agreed with Matilda. "At this point, we will look for anything we can and make notes. We don't know where it could lead. There's a pen and some paper on the table for you, Jane. If you find something interesting, speak up."

I did as I was asked. I sat down and wasted no time looking for Gemma Calhoun's Facebook page. "Her privacy settings seem to be high," I said. "I can't see her list of friends. And it appears she has only shared a whole lot of memes."

Matilda leaned across the table. "What sort of memes?"

"Just those silly ones where the color of what you are wearing plus the last thing you ate is your band name," I told her.

Matilda nodded knowingly. "No doubt that's the only public content she has, and she keeps the rest of the content private. She probably posts a lot about goats."

I agreed. "That goat of hers is her Facebook header." I stared at the photo of the goat, her back covered with ribbons.

"She doesn't have an Instagram account, but I found her Twitter account," Matilda said. "There's somebody on Facebook called Horatio Calhoun-Blye."

"Her husband?" I asked.

Matilda shook her head. "I think he's her son. He looks quite young. He has a bright yellow car."

"That doesn't mean he's young, Matilda," Eleanor said. "Older people can have yellow cars."

Matilda rolled her eyes and swung her laptop around to show us a photo of Horatio standing by his car.

I opened my mouth to speak, but Matilda forestalled me. "I haven't found anybody by that name on any other social media."

Something occurred to me. "I know Damon told me it was poison, but did Detective Stirling give any hints as to the type of poison or anything else?"

Eleanor shook her head. "Detective Stirling didn't ask us any questions about guns or knives or anything like that. He did, however, ask us if we were taking any medication and we told him that we weren't."

"And he was quite rude about it," Matilda said, her tone scornful. "He said it was unusual that women of our age didn't take medication. How ageist of him! The nerve!"

I nodded and sipped my coffee before speaking. "Then maybe Gemma Calhoun was murdered by an overdose of prescription medication. Still, I can't understand why Stirling would suspect you if he believes the first time you met her was when you had that slight altercation at the show. Surely, he doesn't think you went somewhere to procure poison to slip to her."

"Hence why he wondered if we were carrying medication around with us," Matilda said. "They obviously haven't identified the poison yet."

"Well, I could ask Wanda Hershberger." I scratched my head. Wanda was an Amish lady whose daughter, Waneta, worked in the medical examiner's office. She had helped us before, but I didn't know if this was pushing things too far, given that Matilda and Eleanor were considered to be suspects. I didn't want to get Wanda's daughter into any trouble.

Matilda nodded. "That's a good idea. So far we only have Horatio Calhoun-Blye on our list of suspects, so we need to find out what he stands to inherit."

"You're right, Matilda," Eleanor said. "I've been googling Gemma Calhoun's name for ages, and it simply brings up plenty of results from goat shows."

"Wait a moment." I jumped to my feet. "What was the name of her goat, the champion one? That lady, Francis, did mention it."

"It's here on the computer." Eleanor pointed to the screen. "Liberty Hill Farm Sweetened Wine."

I nodded. "Then maybe Gemma bred that goat. Try searching for Liberty Hill Farm."

Matilda and Eleanor tapped away at their keyboards as though it were a competition.

Matilda found it first. She swung the laptop around to show me. "There you are! I found it on an image search."

The image showed a sign with bold brass lettering, 'Liberty Hill Farm,' on a black iron gateway flanked by an imposing stone fence. Through the gate in the background of the photo was an impressive house. "There! She *was* wealthy!" Matilda said with satisfaction. "Therefore the main suspect should be the beneficiary of her will."

"Let's get an address," I said. "It should be easy enough to get an address, maybe from one of the online goat magazines."

Both of them tapped away again, but this time Eleanor was the winner. "I found it! Should we go there now?"

Matilda made a strangling sound at the back of her throat. "Go there now? Are you quite mad? No, it's too late at night and it's too dark outside. We'll go there first thing in the morning before Jane has to be at work. What you think, Jane?"

"Sure," I said. "And I think we need to visit Francis."

"Do you think she is the murderer?" Eleanor said hopefully.

"I don't have an opinion either way, but she would know all the gossip about Gemma

Calhoun. I mean, the goat breeders seem to be a rather tight-knit community, so Francis would surely know what was going on."

"That's a really good idea," Matilda said, looking at me with admiration. "Tomorrow, we will question Francis."

6

I awoke at the crack of dawn, having been up most of the night due to the oversupply of caffeine pumping through me. I had gotten to sleep about three in the morning, and now I felt groggy.

Somebody banged on my door. I opened one eye. "Are you awake, Jane? Let's go!" The voice was Eleanor's.

I dressed and staggered to the kitchen. I reached for the coffeepot, but Matilda slapped my hand away. "I've made a flask.

The taxi will be here any minute—you can drink coffee on our way to Gemma Calhoun's."

Gemma Calhoun's house was only thirty or so minutes away. The gates were open, but we didn't like to go inside for a closer look. "That house wouldn't be cheap," Matilda said in what was clearly a massive understatement.

I agreed. "We'll have to call Francis. But how do we get her number, and what will you say when you call her?"

"I found her number in the list of goat breeders online," Matilda said, "and I already called her."

I was aghast. "What? You already called her? At this early hour?"

Matilda appeared unconcerned. "She's a goat breeder, Jane." Her tone was lecturing. "Dairy goat breeders have to be up early to milk the goats. I thought you of all people would know that, having been Amish. And didn't you say your family had a milking goat or two when you were a child? You must know that dairy goats require milking twice a day, just like dairy cows."

"Still, I would be annoyed if somebody called me early in the morning, no matter how many goats I had to milk," I said. "And what did you tell her?"

"The truth." Matilda smiled widely. "I told her that Eleanor and I had been taken in for questioning last night. I told her the detective in charge doesn't like us and he was trying to pin the murder on us. I said we needed her help to discover who the murderer really is."

I realized I was frowning hard. "And what did she say?"

"She said we could drop by early. I told her you had to start work at nine."

I didn't know whether to be irritated or to be in admiration of Matilda for organizing everything. "So, do we head there now?"

Matilda looked at her phone. "It's a little early. Let's stay here for five or so minutes, drink some coffee, and keep a watch to see if anybody comes or goes."

I thought her plan a good one. After all, there was nothing else to do. Matilda asked the taxi driver—who no doubt thought we were all a little strange—to park down the road a little way, and she produced a large flask of coffee. I felt halfway normal after consuming a cup and held my cup out for more. "Well, nobody left the house," I said. "Maybe she lived alone."

"Francis would know," Eleanor said. "Now Jane, please keep your wits about you, because Francis could well be the killer."

I drained my second cup of coffee as the taxi drove on. Francis lived a further half hour from Gemma Calhoun's house. Her property was far more modest than Gemma's although it was picturesque, a pretty house nestled at the bottom of a hill in the midst of gorgeous, green rolling hills.

The driver left us outside the house. I got out and headed to the front door, but Matilda put her hand on my arm to restrain me. "She might be in the milking shed there," she said, pointing over her shoulder.

She was right. We were halfway to the milking shed when Francis came out. She was wearing old, casual clothes and a worried expression. Still, she offered us a weak smile. "That was good timing," she said. "I've just finished the milking."

"Do you have to milk many goats?"

"Only five does," she said. "Oh, a doe is a female goat, in case you didn't know."

Something occurred to me. "What will happen to Gemma Calhoun's goats, um, does? Who is milking them?"

Francis chuckled. "She didn't milk her own goats. Gemma never liked to get her hands dirty. She paid somebody to do it for her. Don't worry about her goats. Anyway, would you like some coffee? Maybe a cold drink?"

I didn't want to risk becoming over-caffeinated again, and I'd already had two cups of coffee in the car. I was really in the mood for some meadow tea, but I knew *Englischers* wouldn't have any, so I opted for coffee as well. We all thanked her and followed her inside.

The private deck led to the dining area. It, in turn, led past a movable island to a spacious kitchen. I admired the hardwood flooring. We sat around the big wooden table in the kitchen while Francis brewed the coffee.

Francis placed a steaming pot of coffee on the table and set a plain white coffee cup in front of each of us. She handed me one, and I immediately noticed the large chip in the rim. In the middle of the tray was a plate of cookies.

Before sitting down, Francis reached into a narrow drawer in the table and produced a photo album. "This is Liberty Hill Farm Sweetened Wine," she said. "This is where she won the Junior Champion Goat at the state show." She shoved the photo under our noses. "And here are her milk test certificates."

I had no idea how to read a milk test certificate, but I said, "Wow, that's fantastic."

Francis beamed from ear to ear. "Oh yes, just look at that butterfat content! And the yield! Anyone would think she was a Saanen and not a Toggenburg!"

"Quite so, quite so," Matilda said.

After flipping through every page of the weighty album, Francis put it down and then gestured to the large oil painting of a goat behind her. "And that's Liberty Hill Farm Sweetened Wine there."

I was shocked. "I thought it was one of your goats."

Francis seemed to think my statement rather hilarious. "Oh no! None of my goats are as good as Liberty Hill Farm Sweetened Wine." She chuckled. "In fact, nobody's goat is as good as Liberty Hill Farm Sweetened Wine." She smiled and nodded enthusiastically as she spoke.

Matilda pulled out a notepad and pen. "It's good of you to help us like this, Francis. I know you're busy."

"I can't believe the police suspect you. You didn't even know Gemma!"

"We actually met her briefly when we were leading Gigi into the exhibition building,"

Matilda said, "only we didn't know it was her. She jumped in front of us and said we had no right showing a goat that looked like Gigi."

Francis pulled a face. "Yes, that would be her."

"So, can you tell us everything you know about her?" I asked.

Matilda butted in. "Starting with her son, Horatio Calhoun-Blye? Is that his name? And is he the only sibling?"

Francis nodded slowly. "Yes, he's her only child. Her husband died some years ago, and she didn't remarry."

"As far as you know, is Horatio the only one who would inherit anything?" I asked her.

Francis shrugged. "I don't know of anybody else. I only know the local gossip and that sort of thing."

"Gossip?" Eleanor prompted her.

Francis fidgeted with her coffee cup, so I added, "Anything at all you can tell us could be really helpful. Poor Eleanor and Matilda are awfully upset about being questioned for hours last night."

My words must have done the trick. Francis twirled her coffee cup around and then said, "I don't know if this is true, but everyone said Gemma was having an affair with Digby Thompson. He's another goat breeder, you see. He was also opposed to the Any Other Variety class at the show. He and Gemma were the only two who were opposed to it. Everybody else was in favor. They were both furious when the motion in favor was passed."

"Then when you say affair, I assume he was married, since Gemma wasn't?"

Francis nodded. "That's right. His wife's name is Paisley." Her nose wrinkled. "She's not a very nice woman, that one. She and Gemma were like peas in a pod."

I nodded and shot her a smile of encouragement. "And do you know of any other relatives or any other employees? Like who did the goat milking for her?"

"I can't remember the name of the guy who did her milking, but he was also her pool boy. Rumors were she was having a relationship with him too. Still, those could have just been malicious rumors because nobody liked her. Anyway, it seemed the pool boy did anything she asked. It's not often you see a pool boy milking somebody's goats."

I had to agree with that.

"And did Gemma have any other friends? Like actual friends of the female variety?" Matilda asked.

"Not really." Francis bit her lip. "There was Cynthia, although they had a falling out a few months ago."

My ears pricked up. "They had a falling out?" I repeated. I wrote down Cynthia's name and underlined it a few times.

"Do you know what the falling out was about?" Matilda asked.

Francis shook her head. "Not a clue. Cynthia wasn't a goat breeder, but she used to go to goat shows with Gemma. They always seemed like really good friends, but suddenly Cynthia stopped going to goat shows, and people said they'd had a serious falling out. Still, Cynthia was at the goat show the other day."

"And you said Cynthia isn't a goat breeder?" I asked.

"No, she's not a goat breeder. She hadn't been to a goat show with Gemma for some time. Like I said, the two of them had some sort of a falling out. I have no idea what it was all about."

Matilda took over the conversation. "Do you happen to know if Gemma was on any sort of medication?"

Francis looked blank. "Medication?" she repeated.

Matilda nodded. "Did she have a heart condition? Diabetes? Or anything else that you can think of?"

Francis shrugged. "I don't know. You would have to ask her son, Horatio. I do know that she liked to drink. She always carried a hip flask with her. I think it was full of gin. She was always drinking from it. If you ask me, she had a drinking problem. Everybody said so."

I wrote down the word 'gin' and underlined it several times as well.

"So did she always carry this hip flask with her?" Matilda asked.

"I assume so. Ask any of the other goat breeders. Everybody knew about it. She was always sipping from it." She set her coffee cup down hard. "Is that how she was murdered? They said it was poison. Did somebody slip some poison into her hip flask?"

"Yes, it's entirely possible," Matilda said. "Only we have no idea of the poison, and the detective didn't give us any clues when he questioned us last night. Would there be any sorts of poisons that could be lying around at a goat show?"

Francis's hand flew to her throat. "Oh no, of course not! A goat might eat it. Oh, don't get me wrong—I know people say goats will eat anything, but that's simply not true. Goats are, in fact, very picky eaters. They are browsers, not grazers, so they like to eat things like willow branches and trees rather than grazing in a nice field that a horse or a cow would like. In fact, goats would be less likely to eat something poisonous than any other animals, but I suppose it is possible that a goat could eat something poisonous."

As she continued to talk at length in a monotone about what goats would and would not eat, I zoned out. It seemed the hip flask was probably the method of poison. But was it a long-term poison or short-term? I figured the poison had been administered in a large dose just before the victim had died, because she seemed full of life when she was yelling at Matilda and Eleanor. Still, not many poisons can kill so rapidly.

And as for suspects, we already had a few, so things were looking up. Gemma's son, Horatio, probably stood to inherit, and as Gemma had been having an affair, both her lover and her lover's wife were suspects. There was her friend, Cynthia, who was at the show at the time of the murder. And then there was the pool boy who also milked the goats. He maybe stood to inherit something as well. I looked up sharply when somebody said my name.

"Sorry, I was deep in thought. I didn't hear what you said."

Matilda tapped my hand. "Francis has just told us that the pool boy is multi-talented."

Francis interrupted her. "I don't know whether he's actually multi-talented. It's just that I heard he has several part-time jobs."

Matilda nodded. "Yes, he milks the goats, and he's the pool boy, but he also runs classes in town for Pet Protection animals."

"Oh." I didn't know what else to say. I had no idea where this was going.

"But don't you see?" Eleanor's voice rose to a high pitch. "We have the perfect opportunity to question him."

I was completely at a loss. "I'm sorry, I'm really not following."

Eleanor clapped her hands for attention. "I'm going undercover. I'm going to enroll Mr. Crumbles in the pool boy's Pet Protection classes."

7

"Maybe we should pretend that we're Amish people," Eleanor said. "Cynthia wouldn't be suspicious of Amish people."

"But it would take forever to get there in a buggy," I said.

Thankfully, Matilda agreed with me. "Honestly Eleanor, we don't have a week!"

"It wouldn't take a week," Eleanor protested. "And we wouldn't have to spend any more money on taxis."

Matilda put her hands on her hips. "It might as well take a week! Let's just call another taxi."

Thankfully, Eleanor agreed. Matilda and Eleanor had decided we should question Cynthia, Gemma's best friend. When I asked what their plan was, they had told me to leave it to them, and they had advised me to go along with whatever they said. That was fine with me. I would have rather stayed at home, but it was clear I had no choice.

I was on the front porch waiting for the taxi, when Matilda and Eleanor walked out of the door. I gasped. They were both wearing deerstalker hats with the word 'Press' emblazoned across the top. "Are you both pretending to be Sherlock Holmes or something?" I asked when I had recovered from the shock.

"Don't be silly, Jane. We're obviously from the press." Matilda winked and pointed to her hat.

"Does anybody, even journalists, actually wear hats like that?"

Matilda did not seem concerned. "I have no idea, but I'm sure Cynthia doesn't either."

"But she might not want to talk to the media about her best friend's death."

"We intend to tell her that we're from a goat magazine," Matilda countered.

"But Francis said Cynthia didn't like goats."

"Exactly! That will make her less suspicious of us."

I resisted the urge to roll my eyes. The taxi had arrived, and I knew I might as well save my breath. Once Matilda and Eleanor had their minds made up, there was absolutely nothing I, or anybody else, could do about it. I resigned myself to that fact and climbed into the taxi.

Cynthia's house was an hour away. It would definitely have taken a few hours in a buggy.

Besides, I had no wish to go in disguise as an Amish person to question a murder suspect. I had done it before and had no intention of doing it again.

After I paid the taxi, we made our way up to the front steps of the house. The house was nowhere near as grand as Gemma's house, but it was nice, painted in a pretty shade of yellow with a white porch.

Matilda knocked on the door. For a moment, I wondered if maybe Cynthia wasn't home and then I also wondered that if she was home, she might tell us to leave immediately.

The door opened to reveal a well-dressed woman. Waves of French perfume emanated from her. "What can I do for you?" she said rather curtly.

"I'm terribly sorry to call unannounced," Matilda said in soothing tones, "but the magazine only gave us your address. They didn't give us any phone numbers for you. That's why we took it upon ourselves to risk dropping by. I hope you don't mind."

Cynthia frowned deeply. "What's this about?" She gestured to the hats. "You're from a newspaper?"

"We're from one of the dairy goat magazines," Matilda told her. "The editor wants us to do a wonderful story on dear Gemma Calhoun and have her on the cover of our magazine. The committee said you were her dearest friend, so we wanted some information about her."

"All right then, please come in." Cynthia showed us into her living room. It was quite shabby chic with chalk painted furniture side by side with antiques. Items of antique Victorian glassware sat on sideboards all around the room. "You don't have a cat," Matilda said.

Cynthia looked startled as though she had been accused of something. "Why no, I don't. How did you know?"

"Because a cat would have knocked over your some of glassware," Matilda said.

Cynthia relaxed a little and chuckled. "May I offer you a drink?"

"Coffee please," Matilda and Eleanor said in unison.

"Any sort of herbal tea if you have some," I said.

Her nose wrinkled with obvious disgust. "I'm afraid I don't. Would you prefer something alcoholic?"

"Coffee will be fine for me then, thank you."

She gestured to the large grandfather clock by the staircase. "I'm afraid I can't give you long."

She brought my coffee into the room along with Matilda's and then returned with a coffee for Eleanor and what looked like some sort of alcoholic drink for herself, maybe a sherry. "I feel bad drinking alone, but Gemma's death has been a terrible shock," she said.

Matilda pulled a pen and a notepad from her purse. "What can you tell us about Mrs. Calhoun? We know how much she loved her goats."

"Oh yes, her goats," Cynthia said. "That was the one thing we didn't have in common. I'm not an animal lover, you see, and Gemma did love her goats."

"Did she have any other pets?" I asked.

"Oh no, definitely not." Cynthia shot me a long look. "She didn't like inside animals. She always said goats weren't pets; they were livestock. Still, she did love those goats."

"Well, her goats were highly successful," Matilda said. "She was the most successful Toggenburg breeder in these parts."

Cynthia took a big gulp of her sherry. "Yes, indeed she was. I still can't believe she's dead." She wiped her hand over her forehead. "It's all been very distressing, especially with that detective questioning me."

"Why did the detective question you?" I asked her.

"Because I was there at the goat show. He told me he was questioning everybody who was there in case they saw something."

"Did you see something?"

She shook her head. "No. I was watching the goat show."

"Yes, we were questioned too," Matilda said.

"Were you at the show?" Before anyone could answer, she continued, "Oh yes, of course you were at the show because you're from the goat magazine."

"Yes, and..." Eleanor began, but Matilda shot her a quelling look, and she stopped speaking. I expect Eleanor had nearly admitted that they were showing a wild goat.

"It mustn't have been much fun watching the goat show when you don't like goats," I said.

"Yes, it was rather tedious. But Gemma was obsessed with her goats. I thought I should go to support her even though we'd had a falling out a while back and had only recently become friends again."

"Oh, what was the falling out about?" I said in the most even tone I could muster.

There was a long hesitation. I almost thought she was going to ignore my question, but she spoke after a lengthy interval. "Long story short, Gemma didn't like my taste in men. So, is the story going to be about Gemma's murder or about her goats?"

Matilda pretended to look shocked. "Oh goodness me, it's not about her murder, of course. We do work for a goat magazine, you understand, not a sensationalist newspaper."

Cynthia nodded slowly. "So, you want to know what Gemma was like as a person?"

"Yes, as a friend." Matilda leaned forward. "Everybody knew her as a highly successful goat exhibitor, but most of our readers did not know her as a person. Our magazine has a state-wide readership."

Cynthia went to the kitchen and came back with another full glass of sherry. "Gemma was a very good friend. She was a fun person. She had a lot more money than I did, and she was generous. She used to give me lovely things as gifts."

"Before you had the falling out," I said.

She narrowed her eyes. Clearly, she found my mention of the falling out suspicious, or at the very least, distasteful. "Yes," she said. To Matilda, she said, "You can write down that Gemma was a very generous person. I'm fully aware that a lot of people didn't like her, but they didn't know her like I did. She might not have been nice to everybody, but she was kind and generous to her friends. She was a wonderful person."

Matilda scribbled away on her notepad. "That's very helpful. Thank you for your time. We're terribly sorry to intrude upon you like this. We won't quote you, of course."

Cynthia waved one hand at us. "Feel free to quote me saying Gemma was a very generous person. I can't believe she's gone. I hope the police catch whoever did it."

"Do you have any idea who would want her dead?" I asked.

"Nobody, of course." She drained the rest of her sherry in one gulp.

"*Somebody* obviously wanted her dead, because she was murdered," I pointed out.

Cynthia stood up. Her face was white and drawn. "I don't know who it was. Gemma and I had only just gotten back in touch, so maybe she had business dealings that went bad. Perhaps she was having an affair. Don't quote me on that, of course."

"No, of course not. As I said, it's a goat magazine, and we don't intend to mention Mrs. Calhoun's murder at all," Matilda told her, her tone reassuring.

"I'm sorry to bring it up," I said. "I simply volunteered to accompany Matilda and Eleanor here. They're the ones who are interested in goats. I'm not. I watch all those crime shows on TV, and that's why I've asked about her murder. I hope I haven't upset you."

"No, no, you haven't," she said, running her hands through her hair. "I haven't told you anything that I haven't told the police. I told the detective I was fairly certain Gemma was having an affair."

"I'm the one who took the wild goat to the show and entered her in the Any Other Variety class," Eleanor blurted out before Matilda could stop her. "She ate the judge's beard."

Cynthia's face relaxed into a smile. "I heard about that. It must've been quite funny."

"Not for the judge," Eleanor said.

Matilda stood up too. "Thanks for your time. I'm sorry about your friend."

Cynthia nodded and showed us out. I called a taxi on my cell phone while Eleanor and Matilda whispered to each other.

"The taxi will be here in five minutes," I said. "What do you make of that?"

"Interesting she said Gemma was having an affair," Matilda said. "Francis told us it was with Digby Thompson. We must follow up that lead."

"Not until after we take Mr. Crumbles to the Pet Protection classes," Eleanor said. "I wonder how the trainer will teach him to bite on command?"

8

It was with some trepidation that Matilda, Eleanor, and I caught a taxi to Aaron Alexander's Pet Protection training classes. Even Mr. Crumbles looked worried. I had no idea how long the police would require my car. I hadn't heard from Damon, but when I did, that was going to be the first question I asked him.

The taxi driver's expression was still shocked when we paid him and got out of the taxi. The next shocked expression I saw was worn by a rather large dog. The dog presently recovered, and his expression turned to menacing as we approached him. I didn't recognize the breed of dog, but he was large and shaggy and somewhat resembled a bear. A low humming growl emanated from his throat as Eleanor led Mr. Crumbles along the path toward him.

The owner turned around, and at the sight of Mr. Crumbles, tightened his grip on his dog's leash. When Mr. Crumbles drew level with the dog, he hissed and swiped at the dog, which yelped and ran behind his owner's legs.

I bit back a smile.

"That must be the trainer." Matilda nodded to a tall, well-built man.

"How do you know?" I asked her.

Matilda held up her fingers. "One, he doesn't have a dog. Two, he's very good-looking. Three, I imagine Gemma Calhoun would want a young, good-looking man as her pool boy."

I had to agree. "You do have a point."

I had wondered how Eleanor was going to broach the subject with the trainer, but she marched straight up to him. "Aaron Alexander?"

He swung around and regarded the scene before him with obvious horror. "Yes?" he said, staring fixedly at Mr. Crumbles.

"I've come to enroll in your class."

The man's jaw dropped open. "Excuse me?"

"I've come to enroll in your class," Eleanor repeated.

"But, but, this is for Pet Protection dogs," he stammered.

"Your Facebook page says it's for Pet Protection animals. You can't legally oppose having a cat here. That's speciesist."

Aaron's jaw continued to work furiously. Finally, he said, "If you've got the money, I won't refuse you, but I can't promise you any results."

Eleanor handed him some bills. He flipped through them and then smiled. "Sure, you can join in, but I don't like to take your money."

Eleanor simply shrugged and gave Mr. Crumbles a treat.

"Come over here, everybody," he said. "Give the cat a wide berth."

Mr. Crumbles turned around and hissed at the owners, and their dogs all took a step backward.

Aaron then made a speech, which to me was long and rather boring, about the different types of philosophies and training methods of pet protection. "And so the whole point of this is that your pet protection animal is not a guard dog but rather a pet that will protect you should you need it. I hope I have made the distinction clear."

A murmur of agreement went up amongst the people.

"Most people think their dogs—err, and cats —will protect them should they be attacked, but that is rarely the case. It requires specialist training, and it all hinges upon the solid foundation of normal obedience training," he continued. "I want to see you all on board with this. Sure, I know it's the beginners' class, but your dogs need basic obedience training before we can start. Make a circle around me now." He gestured expansively in a circle around himself.

The owners led their dogs in a circle.

"So far so good," I whispered to Matilda.

"Sit!" Aaron yelled.

"Cats don't sit," Eleanor protested.

Aaron walked over to her. "Of course, cats sit," he said. "I don't know what you mean."

"They don't sit on command because they're cats," Eleanor said in a painstaking tone. "They only sit when they want to sit."

Aaron was clearly entirely exasperated. He drew the back of his hand across his forehead. "And that is why cats aren't suitable for Pet Protection training."

"But Mr. Crumbles leads well. It's only that he doesn't want to sit on command. Besides, he's already saved our flatmate there, Jane, from three murderers."

Aaron's jaw dropped open once more. "Excuse me?"

"Is there something wrong with your hearing, young man?" Eleanor said loudly. "Mr. Crumbles has saved our flatmate there, Jane, from three murderers." She yelled, so I assumed everybody in the park heard her.

Aaron looked at me. "Is that right?"

I hesitated. "Well yes, but I don't know if it was deliberate as such. It's just that ..."

Eleanor interrupted me. "How can you say that, Jane? Mr. Crumbles is very clever. I'm certain it was not a coincidence that he saved you, but I admit I'm not so certain about him flying off the stripper's pole."

"The strippers pole?" I'm sure Aaron wanted further clarification, but he turned back to the others. "Walk on!" he called out.

He spent a few more minutes putting the dogs and Mr. Crumbles through their paces. He seemed amazed that Mr. Crumbles could stay on command and would also go to Eleanor on command.

"Can we sit on a park bench?" Matilda said. "Standing here is making my legs ache."

I looked about and spotted a park bench under a tree. "How about over there?"

Soon we were both sitting on the bench, watching Mr. Crumbles. "I don't know what's going to happen when they reach the training where he has to run and attack somebody and bite their arm," I said with a chuckle.

Matilda laughed too. "Oh, I'm sure Eleanor won't bring him back after today. This is just a way to question the suspect without him being suspicious."

I thought a cat turning up at Pet Protection training session was exceptionally suspicious in itself, but I wasn't about to point that out. Thankfully, the training finally came to an end, and Matilda and I hurried over to Eleanor. She was deep in conversation with Aaron.

"I must say, I'm impressed by your cat," he said. "Did you do all the training yourself?"

Eleanor nodded. "Sometimes my sister, Matilda, helped me."

He looked at me. "And did he really save you from three murderers?"

I thought I had better explain. "The first time, a murderer was trying to strangle me, when Mr. Crumbles knocked something onto his head from a high shelf. The second time, well, you see, Matilda and Eleanor put a stripper's pole in the middle of our apartment."

Matilda interrupted me. "It was just for exercise."

Eleanor nodded vigorously. "Matilda and I actually don't work as strippers, not professionally."

Aaron turned pale. I pushed on. "Eleanor had trained Mr. Crumbles to slide down the pole, and he flew off it and hit the murderer in the stomach. The third time, Mr. Crumbles ran around the murderer's legs and trapped him with his leash, because I shook the bag of cat treats."

His eyebrows shot skyward, and he appeared to be having trouble speaking. Finally, he said, "That's amazing. Most people haven't been around one murder in their lifetime, but you have been around three!"

Matilda seized the opportunity. "Four actually. We showed our goat at a goat show the other day, and somebody was murdered while we were there."

Aaron gasped. Before he could speak, Matilda pressed on. "We're not show goat breeders or goat show exhibitors or anything like that, but we did rescue some wild goats, and we thought it would be fun to put one in the Any Other Variety class. When we arrived, a woman barred our way and yelled at us that we had no right showing a goat like that. She turned out to be the woman who was murdered."

"That's right," Eleanor said. She scooped and picked up Mr. Crumbles, who purred loudly.

"And last night the police took us in for questioning, didn't they, Matilda?"

Matilda took a tissue out of her purse and wiped a pretend tear away. "Yes, it was terrifying. I mean, why would we murder her? We only ever saw her for a little more than a minute, and we had never met her before. That's hardly a motive to murder someone."

"And the police have impounded my car looking for evidence," I added. "I drove Matilda and Eleanor to the goat show, but I was sitting in the car when the woman appeared and yelled at them. The whole thing is entirely bizarre."

"She was my boss!" Aaron exclaimed.

Matilda and Eleanor gasped. They were quite good actresses. "What an *amazing* coincidence," Matilda said.

Eleanor nodded. "It's a small world, isn't it? Just like Kevin Bacon."

"Kevin Bacon?" Matilda snapped. "What's Kevin Bacon got to do with anything?"

"You know, seven degrees of separation. It's all about Kevin Bacon, how somebody knows somebody who knows somebody else who knows somebody famous. Kevin Bacon was in a movie about it."

Matilda waved her arms in the air. "Don't be silly, Eleanor! Kevin Bacon wasn't in a movie about it. It was a game. And it was six degrees, not seven."

Thankfully, Aaron spoke before the bickering could escalate. "The police questioned me too."

"Then maybe we shouldn't feel sad about being questioned, Eleanor," Matilda said. "Maybe they're questioning everybody who'd ever met Mrs. Calhoun." To Aaron, she said, "You said you worked for her? Were you training her dogs?"

Aaron chuckled. "She didn't have any dogs. I used to milk her goats, and I cleaned her pool on a regular basis."

I had intended to leave the questioning to Matilda and Eleanor, but something he said bothered me. "You *used* to milk her goats. You're not milking her goats anymore?"

He shook his head. "I'm afraid not. Her son gave me notice last night."

"For what reason?" Matilda asked.

Aaron shrugged. "I have no idea. I had just gotten back from the police questioning me. Horatio banged on my door and said I had to be out of there in forty-eight hours. He told me to milk the goats on time the following morning and then never again. He did say he would pay me what he owed me, but I had to be gone."

"That's terrible!" Matilda said. "Who's going to milk the goats now? Maybe Horatio will."

Aaron seemed to find Matilda's remark awfully funny. "Horatio doesn't know the first thing about goats. Gemma didn't even know how to milk a goat. She just liked the glory of taking goats to shows, but she didn't really know much about them. She always had advice on what to do."

"But didn't she breed that champion show goat?" I asked him.

He nodded. "Sure, but only because she paid a small fortune for the goat's mother, and got expert advice on the buck she should breed her with. She wasn't an animal person, and Horatio is even less so. I don't think he's ever gotten his hands dirty." He broke off for a moment and looked downcast. "Maybe he thinks I *did* murder his mother and doesn't want a suspect on the property. I don't know where I'm going to find any accommodation at such short notice."

"Do you have a dog?" Matilda asked him. "Or any pets?"

"No, I wasn't allowed to have a dog because I was living on Gemma's property," he said.

"I know of a vacant apartment that might suit you," Matilda said.

9

Eleanor let out a shriek. "Jane, it's your car!"

I stumbled out of the shower and hastily threw on my clothes and some make-up. I was running late. I grabbed my purse and ran down the stairs.

I expected a uniformed officer would be returning my car, so I was surprised to see Damon sitting in Matilda's old Adirondack chair on the porch.

I hurried over to him while Matilda and Eleanor beat a hasty retreat back inside the house.

"Thanks so much for bringing my car back," I said.

Damon smiled at me. "I'm sorry that Carter took it in the first place."

At least, that was what I guessed he said. His Scottish accent was even thicker today.

Damon pushed on. "I'm glad you're here. I was just about to catch a taxi."

"I wouldn't hear of it! I'll drive you. I have to go to work now anyway, and Matilda and Eleanor are showing someone Rebecca's apartment."

Damon chuckled. "Does Rebecca know?"

"No, she doesn't." I was not too happy about Matilda and Eleanor suggesting that Aaron see Rebecca's apartment. After all, he was a suspect in a murder case, and we didn't know anything about him. Still, I figured Rebecca would ask for references. I would have time to warn her before he arrived. I looked up to see Damon regarding me strangely.

"Is anything wrong?"

I gestured to my car and raised my eyebrows. "Um, well, the police took my car. Matilda and Eleanor were questioned."

Damon laid his hand on my shoulder briefly before snatching it away and looking awkward. "Don't let it trouble you. I'm sure Carter will soon turn his attention to somebody else."

"I hope you're right," I said.

"So, what have you been doing lately?"

I knew he was fishing as to whether we had been investigating the murder. "Eleanor took Mr. Crumbles to obedience class." It wasn't exactly a lie, but I didn't want to mention pet protection in case he put two and two together and realized we were, in fact, looking into the murder.

Still, he shot me a penetrating look. "Jane, are you investigating?"

I had cleared my throat. "Investigating? Why, do you think I need to investigate? Do you really think Detective Stirling suspects us?"

Damon's eyes narrowed, but before he could say anything, Matilda and Eleanor hurried out of the door. "Come on, Jane, we're going to be late," Matilda said.

I suspected she had overheard what Damon said and had come to my rescue.

When we went to the car, Damon tried to insist that either Eleanor or Matilda sit in the front, to no avail. Soon, I was driving with Damon sitting next to me. It was quite pleasant. I could get used to this, although no one spoke and the heavy silence was most uncomfortable.

I left Damon at the police station after thanking him again for bringing back my car.

He winked at me. "I'll be in touch soon." With that, he was on his way, and I continued down to Rebecca's Amish cupcake shop.

I parked the car around the back. Rebecca's buggy wasn't there, so I had plenty of time after all. I unlocked the door, and we all walked inside.

I set about getting everything ready for opening, with Matilda and Eleanor helping me. "Aaron will be here soon," Matilda said after she and Eleanor had spent a good five minutes arguing whether Shoo-fly pie cupcakes or Amish sour cream spice cupcakes should take pride of place in the display cabinet.

"Rebecca might not be too happy about that," I said.

Rebecca stepped through the door. "I won't be too happy about what?"

I opened my mouth to speak, but Matilda beat me to it. "We met a nice young man."

Eleanor waved her aside. "He doesn't have any pets, but he's very kind to animals. He does train pets for a living, although he's also a pool boy and goat milker. Or rather he was, and that's why he needs the apartment."

Rebecca clutched her head with both hands. I knew that feeling well. "I don't understand."

Matilda shot Eleanor a quelling look. "Of course, you don't understand! Allow me to explain it properly. A nice young man by the name of Aaron Alexander is looking for an apartment to rent. He has just been given notice from his current accommodation. It was quite unexpected."

"Why, was it something he did?" Rebecca narrowed her eyes.

"No, it wasn't his fault. His employer died," Matilda said.

"Actually, she was murdered, and that's why the detective came to take us from dinner last night," Eleanor supplied. "But we don't think he did it."

Matilda folded her arms over her chest. "Of course we don't think he did it! Otherwise, we wouldn't have told him about your apartment."

"That's not to say we don't suspect him," Eleanor added. "It pays to be suspicious of everybody. Not especially everybody—we know Jane didn't murder the vic, and we know Matilda didn't do it, but even if he *is* the murderer, I'm sure he won't murder you, Rebecca."

Rebecca looked too shocked to speak, so I thought I had better say something. "Look, this is a bad idea," I said. "When he arrives, we'll just tell him this has been a mistake."

"I *am* looking for somebody to rent the apartment," Rebecca said.

"But what if he's the murderer?" I said, shocked that she didn't seem to be taking this seriously.

"Then I'm sure *Gott* would know that."

I took a deep breath and let it out slowly. An Amish principal was *Gelassenheit*, a rarely spoken word but one to which the Amish adhered. It was hard to explain, but part of the concept embraced the fact that the Amish surrendered to God's will. They believed all things worked together for good.

"It wasn't his fault he was evicted from his current accommodation," Matilda said. "The victim's son, Horatio, inherits everything, and he doesn't like goats. The victim had dairy goats. Aaron lived in a cabin on the property and used to milk the goats, but now Horatio doesn't need Aaron any more."

"I'll meet him soon enough," said Rebecca. "Are you certain he doesn't have any pets?"

Matilda shook her head. "He wasn't allowed to have pets where he lived before. He *is* very good with goats, though."

"I will not allow him to keep a goat in my apartment!" Rebecca's tone was firm.

"I'm sure he doesn't want to," Matilda said, exchanging glances with Eleanor.

Aaron was five minutes late. He hurried through the door, apologizing. "I'm so sorry I'm late," he said. "Horatio told me I had to leave right away. He said I could send for the furniture and other stuff later. He wanted me out of the way before the goats left."

"So exactly what *is* happening to the goats?" I asked him.

He shrugged. "I assume he sold them."

"And they're leaving today?" Matilda asked. "Horatio found a buyer awfully fast, didn't he?"

Aaron shook his head. "They are top show goats, and I assume there's a waiting list of people who want them."

Rebecca came out of the back room. Aaron looked surprised to see her. I realized we hadn't told him she was Amish. He nodded to her. "Pleased to meet you, Mrs. Yoder," he said. "The ladies did tell me the apartment was above an Amish cupcake store, but I didn't realize the owner was actually Amish."

Rebecca chuckled. "You must be Aaron. They've been telling me about you. Come and see the apartment."

I wanted to go with her, so I said to Matilda, "Matilda, could you mind the shop?"

"Sure," she said and then turned to Eleanor. "Eleanor, mind the shop, won't you." She said it as a command and then hurried after us, leaving a sputtering Eleanor behind.

Aaron was clearly impressed with the apartment. "It's bigger than I thought," he said. "I didn't ask how many bedrooms it had, and there are three. I'm not sure I could afford it. I do have my own business which pays well, but I was also getting free accommodation on Gemma's property in exchange for my work. Now, I'm solely relying on my business."

When Rebecca told him the price, he was visibly relieved. "I can afford that. That's quite reasonable, especially for three bedrooms. Are you sure?"

Rebecca nodded. "But it would have to be only you. You can't sublet it to anybody because it's over my store. I'd rather have someone reliable here, so I'm happy to rent it for less to one person. No parties, mind you. You would have to be quiet."

Aaron was delighted. "You have a deal."

"But if it turns out that you murdered Mrs. Calhoun, then the lease will be broken immediately," Matilda said.

Aaron uttered a nervous laugh, but I knew she wasn't joking.

10

Matilda and Eleanor had convinced me that we needed to speak with Francis face to face. They were certain we would obtain more information from her that way.

And so, after work, I drove Matilda and Eleanor to Francis's farm.

"What if she's in the middle of milking all the goats?" I asked.

"No, it's well after five and they usually milk goats around three," Matilda said. "Honestly, Jane, you should know that."

I cut the engine and stared at her. "How do you know so much about so many obscure things?"

"You'd be surprised," Eleanor said, earning her a glare from Matilda.

"Leave all the talking to me," Matilda said as she jumped out of the car more nimbly than somebody half her eighty plus years.

We headed for the door, but Francis walked outside to greet us. "I thought I heard a car," she said. This time, she didn't invite us in, and we all stood around awkwardly.

"We were hoping you could give us some information about Gemma Calhoun," Matilda said.

Francis hesitated for a moment and then said, "Please come in."

I didn't know if it was my imagination, but I thought her welcome was slightly more chilly than the previous one.

We traipsed inside. This time, Francis showed us into the living room and indicated we should sit on a comfortable couch. She sat opposite us in a rocking chair.

I looked around the room. It was quite homey. Large, ornate, framed pictures of goats wearing champion ribbons covered the walls. The couch and the rocker were upholstered in a matching floral pattern, and magazines lay strewn across the coffee table. There were some gardening magazines mixed with the inevitable goat magazines.

Francis came straight to the point. "How can I help you?"

"We wondered what became of Gemma Calhoun's goats."

Francis gave a little start. "Became of them?" she repeated.

Matilda nodded and pushed on. "Yes, we happened to bump into Aaron Alexander at the park and he told us that Gemma's son, Horatio, had sold all the goats."

"Oh yes, I see what you mean. He must be the goat milker." She folded her hands and placed them on her lap. "I bought them."

"You did?" I said, rather too loudly.

Francis looked somewhat guilty. "Yes, I did. Horatio called me last night and offered them to me at a rather ridiculously low price, but don't tell anybody I said that." She broke off and uttered a nervous laugh.

"Why did he offer them to you rather than anybody else?" Matilda asked her.

She shrugged.

Matilda pushed on. "I thought you didn't like Mrs. Calhoun?"

"*Nobody* liked Gemma," Francis said, "but I doubt her son knew that or even cared. He isn't a goat person, you see. He had no idea of the value of the goats. In fact, I now own Liberty Hill Farm Sweetened Wine herself!"

"And you got her for a song?" I guessed.

She nodded. "But the transfer is signed; it's all perfectly legal. The goats were jointly owned by Horatio and Gemma, and he's signed the papers over to me."

"Why did he jointly own the goats when he didn't know anything about them?" Matilda asked.

"I have no idea. You would have to ask him."

"How many goats did you end up with?" I asked her.

Francis relaxed a little into her chair. "Too many! I have the champion goat, Liberty Hill Farm Sweetened Wine, and two of her daughters, and then another eight goats. I expect I'll sell the other goats at some point. I haven't really decided yet. After all, I'm shocked that Gemma died and then shocked that Horatio offered them to me."

"Why do you think he offered them to you?" Matilda said. "If you could think on that, it might be a great help in solving her murder."

Francis frowned hard. "I don't see how it could be of help, but I kept asking Gemma that if she ever did want to sell Liberty Hill Farm Sweetened Wine, she would give me first offer. I expect she mentioned it to Horatio. Is that any help?"

"Possibly not." Matilda shook her head. "Still, it might be of help later on. I take it you got on better with Horatio than with his mother?"

"That's for sure," Francis said. "I've always gotten along well with Horatio. He always was a nice man."

Eleanor spoke for the first time. "How did you know him if he didn't go to goat shows?"

Francis shifted in her seat. "Horatio *did* go to goat shows. Gemma made him carry stuff for her, that sort of thing. She was a bit of a bully."

Eleanor nodded. "Would you have any idea who would want to murder Mrs. Calhoun?"

Francis pulled a face and inclined her head slightly. "No. I mean nobody liked her, but not enough to kill her, surely."

"What about Horatio himself?" I asked her. "He certainly has the best motive."

Francis was visibly annoyed. Her face turned an unpleasant shade of red. "Motive? No, of course not. Horatio would never kill his own mother."

"Clearly, Mrs. Calhoun was very wealthy, and Horatio is apparently the sole heir as far as we know," Matilda said. "We heard there were no siblings."

Francis took off her glasses and wiped them on her shirt before popping them back on the end of her nose. "No, there are no other siblings, and Horatio did tell me he is the sole heir, but why would Horatio murder his mother? I mean, why now? Gemma hasn't come into any more money recently, and if he was going to murder her, surely he would have done so years ago."

I didn't follow her logic, but I nodded simply to placate her. She certainly did get all riled up at our suggestion that Horatio could be the murderer.

My thoughts turned to Aaron. "What about the young goat milker and pool boy, Aaron Alexander?"

"I guess he's out of a job, isn't he." Her tone was matter-of-fact. "Well, I do my own milking, and I don't need anybody else's help."

"I wasn't suggesting he work for you. I was asking whether you thought he might have a motive to murder Mrs. Calhoun."

Francis quirked one eyebrow. "Are you asking if he was having an affair with Gemma, and then she broke it off with him, so he was hurt and murdered her?"

"Well, no..." I began, but she pushed on.

"Or maybe she found out he was having an affair with her best friend and threatened him. Or maybe he found out she was having an affair with another man and murdered her in a jealous rage."

I was about to protest that I did not mean that at all, when Matilda piped up. "Yes, any of those could be possibilities. Did Aaron have a good relationship with Mrs. Calhoun?"

"I have no idea. She barely mentioned him to me, and I've never met him. Do the police know what killed her yet?"

"Poison," I said.

Francis looked quite put out. "Yes, of course. I mean, I guess everyone knows that, but have they discovered the type of poison it was?"

"If they have, they haven't told us," Matilda said.

Francis nodded slowly. "As far as I know, Gemma didn't have a medical condition, but you never know, do you? Still, if it was simply an accidental overdose of medication, the police wouldn't be carrying on like they are now."

"Have they questioned you?" I asked.

She nodded and once more took off her glasses to wipe them on her shirt. "Yes, a detective came here and made a nuisance of himself. He came right when the goats arrived. I was doing my best to settle them into their new home—goats are very sensitive creatures, you see, and it was stressful for them to arrive at a new place—and all the detective wanted to do was ask me questions. He seemed suspicious that I had Gemma's goats. As if I would murder somebody just to get Liberty Hill Farm Sweetened Wine! How ridiculous. There would be no one left in the goat world if everybody murdered the owner of the goat they wanted." She made a disparaging sound.

"Was it Detective Stirling?" Matilda did not wait for Francis to respond but continued. "He questioned us both, didn't he, Eleanor?"

Eleanor nodded vigorously. "He wasn't very nice. After all, we had only met the victim once and didn't even know who she was at the time. He questioned us for hours and even impounded Jane's car. It seems rather over the top. I'm sorry he gave you a hard time too."

Francis narrowed her eyes. "Yes, it's been quite stressful. I'm hoping I will feel better tomorrow after a good night's sleep. It was a shock that Gemma died when we were there at the show. It was also a shock to get a call from Horatio out of the blue offering me his mother's goats, even though it was a good shock, and then I'm excited to have Liberty Hill Farm Sweetened Wine, but at the same time I feel guilty because I'm excited to have her in spite of the terrible circumstances."

She took a deep breath and then bent forward and put her head in both hands. "Maybe I need therapy." She uttered a rueful laugh.

"It seems the police don't have any real suspects then," Matilda said. "Are you sure Mrs. Calhoun didn't have any enemies?"

"Gemma had plenty of enemies, but I can't think of anybody who would actually want her dead. I mean, it's rather extreme, isn't it?"

We all agreed that it was.

Francis stood up. "Well, if you'll excuse me, ladies, I had better go and check on those goats. The poor things have only been here a few hours, and I want to make sure they all settle in nicely. It's a lot of upheaval for them, you understand."

We followed her out the front door. When we were in my car and safely out of earshot, I said to Matilda and Eleanor, "Do you think she did it?"

"Anything is possible," Matilda said, "and although she protests that she wouldn't murder Gemma just to get Liberty Hill Farm Sweetened Wine, she sure is obsessed with that goat."

11

Matilda leaned over from the back seat and yelled in my ear. "Maybe we should drop by Wanda Hershberger's house now."

"What, now?" My spirits fell. I wanted to get home and enjoy my new house. The investigating was tiring as well as stressful. "We could go early in the morning."

"We need to go there now."

I sighed. "Okay. I hope she doesn't mind."

"She always seems pleased to see us," Matilda said.

I grimaced. "I hope we don't wear out our welcome."

"We don't have to stay for long," Matilda continued. "We just have to ask Wanda to ask her daughter to find out the type of poison used on Gemma."

I waved one hand over my shoulder. "You know I don't like doing that. I think it's an imposition. I know she doesn't seem to mind..." My voice trailed away.

"Why don't you tell her you understand she might not be able to help but ask her to help anyway?"

I was about to suggest that Matilda ask her, but then I realized it would be better coming from an ex-Amish person like myself.

I turned down the long driveway to Wanda's farm. She was in her vegetable garden. She broke into a smile when she saw us. "Oh, I wondered who could be in the car. I don't get many *Englisch* visitors."

"Yes, we only seem to visit when we want your daughter to find out something for us," Matilda said with a laugh.

Wanda chuckled too. "*Nee*, you were kind enough to bring me cupcakes on other occasions."

I nodded. "I don't have any cupcakes this time because we've just been to speak with a suspect."

Wanda gave no indication that she found my words surprising. "You had all better come inside." To me, she said, "You look as though you could use a cup of meadow tea."

"That's for sure!" I said with feeling.

Wanda ushered us inside. As soon as we sat down, she vanished from the room to return soon with a tray of cups and slices of dry bottom Shoo-fly pie. The aroma, both the peppermint of the tea and the molasses of the pie, was heavenly. "Help yourselves," she urged us.

"Matilda and Eleanor seem to be murder suspects this time," I told her. "A detective took them in for questioning, and my car was impounded for a short time."

She nodded. "*Jah*, I know all about it."

I was surprised. "You do?"

She continued to nod. "Waneta told me. She overheard the police talking about it. She was quite concerned that anyone could possibly think the three of you were involved, so she told me something in confidence."

Eleanor leaned forward in her chair. "What was that?"

Matilda was quite put out. "Honestly, Eleanor! Wanda said it was in confidence. That means she can't tell us."

Eleanor's lips pursed. "I know what it means. Do you think I'm a fool?"

Wanda obviously saw the situation was about to escalate, so she quickly said, "*Nee*, Waneta wanted me to tell you. She said it was in confidence, meaning I couldn't tell other people, but she wanted me to tell you."

I could see Matilda was torn between not being right and wanting to find out the information Waneta had for us.

"Waneta knows the type of poison." I said it as a statement, not a question.

Wanda set down her cup of meadow tea. It was a particularly pungent brew, and the fragrance of peppermint wafted toward me. "It was ethylene glycol."

"Car coolant?" Matilda said in shock.

"Exactly."

Matilda's hand flew to her throat. "But Agatha Christie didn't poison anyone with coolant."

I was puzzled. "But what would it taste like? Wouldn't it taste horrible? Why would somebody slip that into someone's drink? I mean, surely there are more effective poisons? How much of it would it take to kill somebody? And what would taste like?" I asked again.

Wanda stood up. "I'll fetch the information."

The three of us exchanged glances but remained silent.

Wanda returned and sat down in her chair. She produced a piece of paper. "Waneta asked me to burn this piece of paper after I read to you, just to be on the safe side," she said.

"Very *Mission Impossible*," Matilda said.

"An impossible mission?" Wanda said, clearly confused.

I hurried to explain. "It was a TV show, now a series of films."

Wanda did not seem interested in the slightest. "Oh, I see." She picked up her glasses from the big German Bible next to her on the small wooden table and pushed them back on her nose. "Ethylene glycol." She looked up at us. "Yes, I already told you that." She looked back down at the slip of paper. "One ounce of ethylene glycol is fatal in humans."

"One ounce!" Matilda exclaimed. "That's about the size of a shot."

Wanda was clearly confused. "A shot?"

"A shot of alcohol," I told her. "It's a measure of alcohol. People drink it in one gulp."

Wanda nodded slowly. "Yes, I see," she said, although the expression on her face showed clearly that she didn't. She looked down at the note and then back up at us with a bright smile. "That's exactly what Waneta has written here. Shot glasses were on the desk in the office where the victim was found. The poison, the ethylene glycol, was found in one of them. Waneta also notes that there was a hip flask of brandy that also contained ethylene glycol, although it appeared hardly any was missing."

"So somebody gave it to the vic as a shot," Eleanor said. "The fact that she had a hip flask shows she was prone to drinking, and obviously whoever killed her knew of her tendency to drink."

"Obviously," Matilda said.

"But what would it taste like?" I said. I tapped myself on the side of my chin. "Still, I suppose people don't taste shots before they swallow them."

"Ethylene glycol is generally sweet," Matilda said. "Maybe it didn't taste all that unpleasant."

"That's true, but what color was it?" Eleanor said. "If it was the bright green ethylene alcohol, I doubt she would have thought it was an alcoholic beverage." She hesitated and then added, "Unless maybe she thought it was absinthe, but people don't do shots of absinthe."

I was wondering how Eleanor knew so much about absinthe, when Wanda spoke again. "Green," she pronounced suddenly. "Waneta also said that the office was at the back of the building and nobody was supposed to be there. That's why there were no witnesses. Will you remember all that so I can burn it now?"

We all said that we would. She crossed to the fireplace, threw it in, and then turned back to us. "I'll burn it later. Was that a help?"

"It was a great help, thank you," I told her. "Please thank Waneta for us. It was very good of her to tell us all this."

"Waneta did feel bad about passing along the information, but she knows that you didn't do it, Jane, and she knows Matilda and Eleanor didn't do it as well. She's worried that the murderer will get away, and she knows the three of you are investigating."

"We don't want anybody to know we're investigating, though," I said.

"Especially not Jane's detective." Matilda chuckled.

"He is not *my* detective," I said and then quickly added, "He's not even on the case. Detective Stirling is the one who impounded my car and took Matilda and Eleanor in for questioning."

A knowing look passed over Wanda's face. I expect Waneta had told her mother what she thought of Detective Stirling's investigation.

We thanked Wanda once more and took our cups into the kitchen. She insisted we take the remainder of the dry bottom Shoo-fly pie with us. "It's wonderful you have a new house, Jane," she said.

"You must come and see it," I said. "Bring Waneta too. You must come over for dinner."

"*Denki*, that would be *gut*."

As we walked away, Eleanor said, "See, I told you I was learning Pennsylvania Dutch. She said, 'Thank you, that would be good.'"

Matilda stopped walking and stomped her foot. "Honestly, Eleanor! Sometimes I think you have completely taken leave of your senses. Obviously, that's what it meant. Anybody would know that. Every time someone says '*Denki*, that would be *gut*,' you always say 'I know what that means.'"

"I do not."

"Yes, you do!"

"In the car, both of you," I said. "We have to go home and figure out what to do next."

"I know what we have to do next," Matilda said. "We have to investigate Horatio." She said the words with relish.

My stomach sank. "I hope that doesn't mean breaking and entering?"

Matilda simply chuckled.

12

I'd had a fairly pleasant night's sleep. The previous evening, we had driven past Horatio's house several times and had not seen anybody. Eleanor had convinced me to drive past in the evening, but no lights were on. Just where was Horatio? We were keen to question him, under a pretext of course, but had not been able to find him.

On the bright side, I had a dinner date with Damon to look forward to. Also, there had been no word from Detective Stirling, which I took as a very good sign

I was sitting by myself, drinking my coffee in peace in the kitchen, hoping that Matilda and Eleanor had given up the idea of investigating, when Eleanor burst into the room. "The funeral is today!"

I jumped, almost spilling my coffee. "Today?"

Matilda stumbled into the kitchen. "Tell me after I have some coffee soup."

Eleanor's nose wrinkled in disgust. "I don't how you can eat that stuff."

"I liked it the first time I had it at Wanda's house," Matilda said. "It's a nice breakfast with the added benefit of caffeine. You should try some, Eleanor."

Eleanor clutched her iPad to her chest and backed away. "No way! Anyway, did you hear what I said?"

"Caffeine first, hearing second," Matilda said. After her breakfast was prepared, she sat down at the kitchen table next to Eleanor.

Mr. Crumbles jumped into Eleanor's lap and looked over at Matilda's food. "You wouldn't like it, trust me," Eleanor said.

"What's this about a funeral?" Matilda said.

"Why, it's Gemma Calhoun's funeral obviously."

Matilda was visibly annoyed. "Obviously! I know that. Why is it today?"

"How would I know why it's being held today?"

I thought I had better intervene. "How did you find out the funeral was today?"

"I joined the Facebook page for the local dairy goat exhibitors and breeders in this area," Eleanor told me. "There was a post earlier this morning that said the funeral is today."

"Isn't it strange that the police would release the body so soon?" I asked them.

Both sisters shrugged. "Not if the police have everything they need, which they obviously do," Matilda said. "It must be cut and dried that the coolant killed her."

"And I think we were right to suspect the son more than anybody else," Eleanor continued, "given that the vic is being cremated."

Matilda tapped her chin. "Aha! Cremation—that's always suspicious. If the murderer has any control over the burial, he or she usually selects cremation to make it harder for the police going forward."

"But you said the police only released her body because they had everything they needed," I protested.

"I'm sure I could quote many cases where the police thought they had everything they needed but later wished they'd still had the body," Matilda said. "Still, as much as we dislike Detective Stirling, he's no fool. He is not as good as your detective, Jane, but I'm sure he knows what he's doing."

I clasped my hands. "Excellent! Well, that settles it then. We'll leave Detective Stirling to get on with his job solving the case, and we'll go back to our usual lives."

Matilda and Eleanor gasped in unison. "Have you taken leave of your senses, Jane?" Matilda said. "I don't trust the man *that* much! No, he's already taken us in for questioning, and until this murder is solved, we are still persons of interest to him. We need to solve this murder and do it as fast as possible."

For once, Eleanor quickly agreed with her. "We need to go to the funeral today."

"I don't know if Rebecca can spare me from the shop," I said, hoping Rebecca wouldn't be able to give me any time off.

"I'm sure she will," Matilda said.

And, much to my dismay, it turned out she was right. Matilda had asked Rebecca if I could attend the funeral. Rebecca had only been too pleased to let me go, despite me wriggling my eyebrows and shaking my head behind Matilda's back.

Rebecca ushered me out of the door. "Things are a little quiet at the moment, and there is no baking that needs to be done. Off you go, Jane."

When we reached the little church, I was surprised to see the number of cars.

"Gemma Calhoun sure was popular," Matilda said. "Or, if not popular, then she was certainly a well-known figure in the dairy goat showing community."

"The murderer will be at the funeral," Eleanor said confidently. "We need to keep our eyes peeled for anybody acting suspiciously."

"Why would anybody act suspiciously at a funeral?" Matilda asked her.

"You know what I mean," Eleanor countered. "It's just a figure of speech. I mean that we need to keep our eyes open for suspects. In particular, we need to keep our eyes on Horatio, the vic's son. As far as we know, he inherits everything. That's a good motive if ever I've heard one."

"It *is* a good motive," Matilda conceded, "but that doesn't mean he's the murderer. He wasn't seen at the goat show, and the shot glasses were in the office, according to Waneta. That means the murderer had to be physically present."

"You're right for once," Eleanor said. "If the ethylene glycol was simply in the hip flask, then it could have been put in at any time. No, the murderer wanted to make sure the vic drank enough, and to do that, the murderer needed to be present while the vic took the shots, or shot as the case may be. Surely Gemma wouldn't have done shots with a stranger. Just because Horatio wasn't seen at the goat show doesn't mean he wasn't there. We really need to look into his alibi."

Matilda nodded. "Yes we do, and we also need to find out..." Her voice broke off. "Jane, here's Damon."

I turned around. "Damon!" I exclaimed. "What are you doing here? I thought you wouldn't be allowed."

Damon looked puzzled. "Wouldn't be allowed?" he repeated.

I was a little embarrassed and shifted from foot to foot. "I mean, didn't Detective Stirling say you shouldn't work on the case?"

Damon chuckled. "Sure, but Carter isn't my boss. He's my partner. I'm not working on the case, but I thought I'd come to the funeral to make sure you weren't investigating."

With that, Matilda took Eleanor's arm and hurried her inside the church.

"Eleanor and Matilda insisted I come to the funeral," I said, and that was the truth, although of course there was more to it than that.

Damon shot me a penetrating look. "Jane, need I remind you how many times you've nearly gotten yourself killed because you've been investigating a case?"

"No, you don't need to tell me," I said. "I was hoping Detective Stirling would have solved the case by now."

Damon leaned forward. "I was hoping the same thing," he whispered. He straightened up and added, "Jane, I wish you'd leave it alone."

"I would rather be back in the cupcake store baking cakes and selling them to customers, but Matilda and Eleanor are upset that Detective Stirling suspects them," I told him.

"He is investigating everyone who was at the goat show."

"He didn't take me in for questioning, but he did impound my car."

Damon sighed. "Let's go inside. Do you mind if I sit with you?"

"I'd be delighted," I said. "So, you're not here officially?"

Damon shook his head but did not elaborate further.

I walked in to see Eleanor and Matilda had already taken their seats at the back of the room, no doubt so they could watch everybody. I slid in and Damon slid in beside me. "Hello, ladies," he said.

"Hello, Damon," they both said in unison.

"Has Detective Stirling solved the case yet?" Matilda asked.

"Not as far as I know, but I'm not on the case." I expected Damon said that so Matilda wouldn't ask any more questions, and it certainly worked.

The church was crowded. Francis walked in but didn't notice us. She walked down the aisle and took a seat several rows in front of us.

I happened to be craning my neck, looking at the door, when Aaron walked in. He caught my eye and walked over to me. "Hello, Jane. Hello, Matilda and Eleanor."

I made the introductions. "Aaron, this is my friend, Damon. Damon, this is Aaron Alexander."

"The apartment is great," he said. "It was very good of you all to tell me about it. And Rebecca is really nice. I can't thank you enough." He smiled and walked away.

I could feel Damon tense beside me. "Who is he?"

"He just leased Rebecca's apartment—you know, the one we all moved out of when I bought the house," I said. I turned to look at Matilda and wiggled my eyebrows in the hopes she would change the subject.

Matilda didn't take the hint. "Yes, Rebecca thinks he's nice," she said.

Damon glared at us. "Why is Rebecca's tenant at the funeral for Gemma Calhoun?"

"Oh, it's the most amazing coincidence," Matilda said. "Eleanor has started taking Mr. Crumbles to Pet Protection classes and Aaron is the instructor."

Damon held up one hand, palm outward. "Wait a minute. Did you say you're taking Mr. Crumbles to Pet Protection classes?"

Eleanor nodded enthusiastically. "Yes. Mr. Crumbles has saved Jane's life on three occasions. We thought we should train him so he would know how to save her life next time in a professional capacity."

Damon wiped his hand across his brow and then shut his eyes tightly. When he opened his eyes, he said, "And so, what did this Aaron Alexander have to do with Gemma Calhoun?"

Eleanor smiled widely. "He just happened to mention how he needed an apartment. He used to work for Gemma Calhoun, and he was renting a cabin on her property because he used to milk her goats."

"And he was her pool boy," Matilda interjected.

"Yes, he also milked her goats and he was her pool boy, but he has his own business in Pet Protection and he just happened to mention that he was looking for an apartment," Eleanor continued, all in one breath.

"He mentioned that to us at the Pet Protection classes," Matilda added. "So we suggested Rebecca's apartment."

Damon by now appeared thoroughly tense. "Let me get this straight. You took your cat to Pet Protection classes so you could question a suspect in a *murder*, and you have organized it so this *murder* suspect has rented Rebecca's apartment. Is that right?"

Matilda appeared unconcerned. "Aaron obviously didn't do it," she said. "He's just a nice young man. And we wanted to help him. We couldn't see him living in his car, could we, Eleanor?"

"Goodness gracious me, of course not," Eleanor said. "He's very good with animals."

"I fail to see the connection," Damon said through gritted teeth.

"He loves animals, so he can't be a murderer," Matilda said.

Damon took a deep breath and let it out slowly. He turned back to the front. After a few moments, he turned to me. "Jane, do you know anything about this?"

"Yes," I said in a small voice.

Damon rubbed his hand over his eyes. "Jane, what if he *is* the murderer? You could have a murderer living in the apartment above your sister Rebecca's cupcake store."

Damon spoke in hushed tones, but Matilda must have had excellent hearing because she leaned across and said, "Don't you worry. He's not the murderer."

Damon would have said something, but the minister stood at the pulpit. I didn't listen to what the minister's words, because I was worried about Aaron. What if he was, in fact, the murderer? I would have to make sure Rebecca was never at the shop alone. Of course, if he was the murderer and he had murdered Gemma, then he must have had a motive. He wouldn't have a motive for murdering Rebecca or a motive for murdering me, for that matter. Still, as much as I tried self-talk to calm myself, my stomach churned at the thought that we might have invited a murderer into Rebecca's apartment.

13

The church was filled with mourners. Several people spoke about Gemma, saying she was a wonderful person and devoted to her goats. I wondered if they were sincere, but then again, I supposed nobody ever said what they really thought of the deceased at the funeral.

I looked around the church but could only see the backs of people's heads. It was hardly the fact-seeking mission I'd hoped for. I noticed Detective Stirling sitting at the other side of the church. A chill ran up my spine as I realized it was more than likely that the murderer was with us right now, perhaps in close proximity to me.

I saw some people shuffle around in their seats and looked out to see a minor scuffle between a man and a woman. After she elbowed him again, he put his head forward. I wondered what that was about and made a note to keep a close eye on them after the service was over.

The service went on for a considerable length of time. The minister returned to the pulpit at the end and said a few more words. We all stood as a mournful hymn played. It brought a tear to my eye, and I hadn't even known Gemma. When it finished, the minister invited everyone to the side room to have fellowship with one another, as he put it, and to remember Gemma.

Matilda elbowed me in the ribs. "That will give us time to mingle and question people," she whispered. I quickly turned to my right, but to my relief, it didn't appear as though Damon had heard her.

He tapped my elbow. "I have to go now, Jane. Remember, no investigating."

I nodded. Damon leaned forward and said, "I'll be in touch about dinner."

I smiled, and he slipped out of the church building. I looked up to see Detective Stirling scowling at me. I held his gaze, and he looked away.

Matilda was only too eager to get to the side room. There was a large stainless steel hot water urn alongside a large glass jar of instant coffee. "Ugh, instant coffee," Matilda said. "It should be illegal."

Eleanor selected a cookie and clutched it to her. "It *is* good in an emergency."

Matilda waved her finger at her. "We're not here for eating, we are here to question suspects. Speaking of suspects, it appears Horatio has left the building."

I looked around but couldn't see him anywhere.

The side room was smaller than I expected, given the size of the church itself. Everyone was hemmed in, so there would be no opportunity for privacy. Still, it would give us the opportunity to overhear people's words. I noticed the man of the couple who had seemed to have an altercation during the service. I walked past them to get a look at their faces. They both looked familiar. That was when I heard the words, "You're here!" and swung around to see Francis frowning at me. Her words sounded like an accusation.

"Yes." I thought it best not to give a reason as to why we were there, although surely Francis realized we were there to question suspects. "It was a lovely service, wasn't it?"

"Yes." Francis regarded me with narrowed eyes. "I see your friends are here with you."

"Yes," I said again. I nodded toward the couple I had seen earlier. I noticed the man's eyes were red and swollen, and his wife appeared tense and angry. "Who are those people?"

"Digby and Paisley Thompson," Francis said.

"Was he close to Gemma?"

Francis took my arm and drew me to the wall. "Yes, he was a little *too* close to Gemma, if you get my meaning."

I nodded slowly. "I see. So, he's married to that woman with him, and he was having an affair with Gemma?"

Francis shrugged. "So the rumors go. I have no idea whether they're true, but he *is* quite upset, isn't he?"

"He is. Maybe he's simply an emotional person, or maybe they were simply good friends."

Francis made a derisive sound. "Good friends, indeed!"

"I know him from somewhere. Wasn't he at the goat show?"

Francis nodded. "Yes, he was. They both were. They breed alpines. They're probably the most successful Alpine show exhibitors in these parts."

"So they wouldn't mind that you got Gemma's goats?"

Francis looked at me as though I were mad. "Of course not! They have Alpines, like I said. They don't want Toggenburgs."

"Oh. And who said that Digby and Gemma were having an affair?"

Francis gestured expensively around the room. "Well, everybody."

"How long has this been going on?"

"I don't know. Months, I suppose."

Digby and his wife were walking our way, Digby ahead of his wife. "So how are the goats settling in?" I said, changing the subject abruptly.

Francis scrunched up her nose. "They're still quite upset."

With that, she nodded to me and walked over to the cookie table. I made my way over to Matilda and Eleanor, casting a look around before I spoke. "Francis told me that Gemma was having an affair with somebody called Digby Thompson. That's him over there with his wife."

"The one who just picked up a cookie?" Eleanor asked.

I nodded. "Yes, that's them. I actually noticed them in the service. She elbowed him hard. I suspect he might have been crying or something like that. Francis said Digby and Gemma had been having an affair for some time."

"Which gives the wife a motive," Matilda said.

I agreed. "Her name is Paisley. They breed goats and they were at the goat show."

"Yes, they do look familiar," Eleanor said. "Wait! Wasn't he the judge?"

"What judge?" Matilda said.

"The one whose beard was eaten by Gigi?"

"He doesn't have a beard," Matilda snapped.

"Obviously not, because she ate it," Eleanor countered.

"I'll go and ask Francis," I said.

I'm sure Francis must have seen me coming, because she headed for the exit. I increased my speed and managed to catch her just outside the door. "Was there something *else* you wanted to ask me?" she said.

"Yes, Digby Thompson. Was he a judge at the show?"

"Yes, he judged the Any Other Variety," Francis said. "Oh yes, of course you wouldn't have recognized him because he had a beard. A rather long beard. He must've shaved it off since the show." She turned to look over her shoulder. "Actually, he looks a lot better now, doesn't he? Maybe Gemma liked him with the beard and now that she's gone, he shaved it off."

"Oh yes, well, thanks for that. I hope the goats settle down soon."

Francis shot me a thin-lipped smile and then hurried away. I went back inside and gave the news to Matilda and Eleanor.

"I knew it was him!" Eleanor said triumphantly.

"You had better keep out of his way. He won't be happy to see you," Matilda said.

I disagreed. "Actually, it gives us a good opportunity to question him."

Matilda and Eleanor looked at me, surprised. "How?" they said in unison.

"Eleanor can go to him and apologize for Gigi eating his beard."

Eleanor looked horrified. "No way! He'll be absolutely furious! He would still be angry with me. I can't possibly do that."

I tapped my chin and thought about it some more. "I have a better idea. His wife had a motive to murder Gemma. Maybe you could find out a time when they won't be together and go to her, pretending you wish to apologize to him but question her instead."

"I don't know about that..." Eleanor began, but Matilda interrupted her.

"That's an absolutely brilliant idea, Jane! Now, we just have to find out where they live or what they do for work and when they will be apart. I've been watching them, and Paisley is clearly annoyed with Digby who isn't able to keep his emotions in check. If she didn't suspect he was having an affair with Gemma before, she obviously does now."

"Well, I suspect her more than anybody," I said. "I hope Detective Stirling has noticed them."

"Yes, he has," Matilda said. "I've been watching him too. And he's definitely been watching them."

"You know, it could have been Digby." I nodded in his direction. He was sipping from a Styrofoam cup, his eyes red and puffy, and looking crestfallen. "Maybe he murdered Gemma, and that's why he is so emotional now."

"Or maybe he and his wife both killed Gemma, and he is remorseful and she isn't," Eleanor said.

I expected Matilda to disagree, but to my surprise, she didn't. "Yes, that's a possibility too," she said. "We don't have a motive. I mean, if Paisley did it out of jealousy, then that's a motive, but we have no motive for Digby murdering Gemma, and we have no motive for the two of them together murdering Gemma. We'll have to do some more digging into this. Did Francis tell you anything else, Jane?"

"Only that that they are Alpine breeders. Oh, and that rumors were that he'd been having an affair with Gemma."

"Okay then, Digby didn't want her goats, and he won't inherit anything," Matilda said. "Speaking of inheritance, Horatio made quite a touching speech about his mother, didn't he?"

"Yes. He did, and so did Gemma's friend, Cynthia."

"Yes, a few people did. Where's Aaron?"

"He left as soon as the service was over," Matilda told me. "I expect he simply came to pay his respects, and he didn't want to speak to Horatio or any of the others. He needn't have worried, as Horatio left directly after the service too."

"That means Aaron has gone back to the apartment," I said in alarm. "What if he's the murderer? I have to get back to the cupcake store right now."

14

I need not have worried. Rebecca had not seen Aaron that day. I had spent the afternoon baking cupcakes: funetti cupcakes with buttercream frosting, salted caramel cupcakes, strawberry cupcakes, and some of the specialist Amish cupcakes: Amish Friendship Bread cupcakes, Amish Sour Cream Spice cupcakes, and Long John Roll cupcakes.

Halfway through the afternoon, I had just finished my normal daily baking duties when Rebecca had come in and told me there would soon be a fundraiser for the widow Troyer's medical expenses. I then busied myself baking for the upcoming fundraiser market.

I also made an Amish Bible Cake to take to Digby ostensibly to apologize for Gigi eating his beard and also as an opportunity to question him.

After we shut the shop, I waited for Rebecca to drive away before getting into my car with the Amish Bible Cake and heading home. Matilda and Eleanor were waiting for me. "The herb garden is already coming along." Matilda nodded to the garden to my right.

I was shocked. "Wow, you've done so much!" Matilda and Eleanor were keen gardeners and used to have a small herb garden in the courtyard adjacent to Rebecca's cupcake store.

"Did you bake a cake for Digby?"

I nodded to Matilda. "I sure did." I opened the car door and made to get it out, but Matilda and Eleanor hurried over to me. "Let's go now."

"Now?" I said. "But I've just finished work for the day."

Matilda jumped into the car. "No time like the present," she said. "You'll be able to relax afterward. We made dinner for you, so you won't have to do a thing, just come home and relax."

"That's nice," I said. I looked up to see Mr. Crumbles looking through the window at me. He appeared to be frowning, although that was his usual expression. I waved goodbye to him and then felt a little foolish for doing so.

"I'll navigate to Digby's farm," Eleanor said. "I'm not sure how we can question him though. I'd rather have a plan than have to play it by ear."

"Actually, something came up today," I told them. "There's going to be a market day soon to benefit the widow Troyer's medical expenses. The bishop told Rebecca about it yesterday. I've been doing a lot of baking for it, and I thought we could ask Digby and Paisley to donate. That will give us a reason to speak with him."

"What's he going to donate? Goat milk?" Matilda said.

"Goat milk soap and goat milk hand cream, of course," Eleanor said. "At least *I* have been doing my research. Digby and Paisley produce all sorts of goat milk items, such as goat milk lip balm, goat milk lotion, and goat milk bath salt."

"They sound nice," I said. "Still, while the fundraiser does give us more opportunity to speak with him, it doesn't give us the opportunity to discover if he was having an affair with Gemma. I mean, we can hardly ask him if he was having an affair with Gemma

Calhoun or ask him if he or his wife murdered her."

"That doesn't matter," Matilda said from the back seat. "We'll just get him talking. It's amazing what people reveal about themselves in general conversation. Take note of everything he says, and we'll discuss it later."

"It would be good if we could speak with him and his wife separately."

"It doesn't really matter," Eleanor said after suddenly yelling, "Turn left here!"

I slammed on the brakes and then turned left. "I had no idea there were so many goat farms around."

Matilda admonished me gently. "I don't think there are many, just those of Gemma, Digby, and Francis."

"That's three," Eleanor said.

"You interrupted me. I was going to mention that there were other goat breeders from the show."

"Turn right!" Eleanor yelled. To Matilda, she said, "You're always exaggerating."

"I am not!"

"Yes, you are. Jane, take the next turn to the left."

"Oh look, we're here," I said. "I hope he won't be angry to see us."

"Even if he is angry, he will pretend to be polite, I'm sure," Eleanor said.

I couldn't see anybody out in the fields. Over to the left was a large barn, which I figured was the milking shed. We walked over to the house and knocked on the door. Digby answered. His eyes widened and then narrowed when he saw Eleanor. "You!" he said. It came out as a hiss.

I thrust the Amish Bible Cake at him. He took it by reflex.

"What's this?" He looked at it suspiciously.

"We have come to apologize for the behavior of our goat," Eleanor said. "Can you ever forgive me? She was a wild goat and I rescued her. I had no idea she would ever do such a terrible thing." She pulled a tissue out of her purse and dabbed at her eyes.

"Poor Eleanor has been most distraught ever since the incident," I said.

His expression softened. "It was kind of you to rescue a goat. Please come inside." He held the door open. Instead of taking us into the big living room that was directly in front of us, he ushered us through a door to the left into a room which I soon realized was an office. It was of medium size with wood-paneled walls. Huge framed photographs of Alpine goats, their backs covered by ribbons, hung on the walls. Over to one side was shelving showcasing a display of the goat milk products.

After we were seated, Eleanor was the first to speak. "It was awfully kind of you to have an Any Other Variety class at the show. I do hope my goat's behavior hasn't prevented such classes at future shows. I do promise I will never take her to another show."

"That would be wise," Digby said.

"She is a naughty goat," Eleanor continued.

Digby's eyes narrowed. "There's no such thing as a naughty goat. There are only naughty *owners*."

Eleanor shifted in her seat. After an interval, she said, "Yes, you're right. We rescued the goat and I selected her to show because she was the tamest goat of them all. The most naughty goat we have is Billy. He has done some terrible things."

"Yes, we won't go into those now," Matilda said. "We rescued fifteen goats, you see."

"It was very kind of you to do so." His words appeared to be genuine, and his expression softened a little more. "So, you have no interest in dairy goats?"

"No, I'm afraid the milking twice a day would be too much for us," Matilda said, "although we do love goats. We love all animals. Goats have such pleasant personalities."

For the first time since we had been there, Digby's face lit up. "Yes, they do, don't they? Goats are absolutely filled with personality, and they have such wonderful senses of humor. Why, I could tell you stories."

I thought I had better bring the subject around to the victim before he did tell me stories. "It was very kind of you to judge the Any Other Variety class at the show."

Eleanor agreed. "Yes, it was very kind, particularly as we were told that there was a lot of opposition to the class."

He nodded slowly. "Yes, dear Gemma didn't want the class to go ahead, and I agreed with her, but after the committee passed it and everybody refused to judge it, I thought I had better put my hand up. It was the right thing to do. Still, Gemma felt I had betrayed her, and now she's gone." His voice cracked.

I thought either he was a wonderful actor or he was genuinely upset that Gemma had died. We needed to turn our attention to investigating his wife. "Yes, it's a sad loss that the whole goat community must feel," I said. "I'm sure you and your wife were very close to Gemma."

He looked alarmed. "My wife?" he repeated.

I nodded. "Yes, they must have been good friends."

He shook his head. "No, because we breed Alpines."

We must have looked blank, because he added, "Gemma bred Toggenburgs and we breed Alpines."

"You were good friends with Gemma though, weren't you?" Matilda said in an innocent tone.

Digby cleared his throat. "Yes." He stood up. That was obviously our cue to leave, so I pointed to the display on the wall. "Your farm produces all these wonderful products?"

He walked over to them and rested one hand on the wooden shelf. "Yes, we've been doing that for years."

"My twin sister is Amish," I said. "The Amish community around here is doing a fundraiser for a widow's medical expenses. Would you be able to donate some products to it? Even a tiny contribution would be wonderful."

"Oh yes, I would be happy to help the community," he said. "You will have to speak to my wife. She handles that side of things."

I couldn't believe our luck. The three of us smiled widely. No doubt Digby felt we were pleased about the donation.

"And when could we speak with your wife?" I asked him.

"I'll go fetch her now."

15

As soon as Digby left the room, we turned to each other. "I don't think he did it," I whispered. "He seems too upset."

"It could be remorse for murdering her, though," Matilda pointed out.

"I'm on the fence about it," Eleanor said. "I don't think he's acting, and I do think he wears his heart on his sleeve. Either he didn't do it and he's genuinely upset that Gemma has gone or he's upset because he knows his wife did it, and he feels guilty because she committed murder due to his affair with Gemma."

"Hopefully, we can find out something from Paisley," Matilda said.

We could hear yelling in the distance. "That doesn't sound good," Matilda said. "Maybe Paisley won't want to speak with us."

Moments later, the office door flung open, and Paisley strode in.

She looked a formidable figure—well-groomed even though she had probably spent the day in the house—with blonde hair slicked back and wearing a string of pearls, a sensible suit, and sensible shoes. She extended her hand. "I'm Paisley Thompson."

I shook her hand. Her grip was particularly firm.

"My husband"—she almost spat the word—"tells me you would like a donation for a fundraiser?"

Matilda nodded. "Actually, we came here to apologize to your husband."

Her brow wrinkled with confusion. "Apologize? Why?"

"Because my goat ate his beard at the show when your husband was judging the Any Other Variety class," Eleanor said.

Paisley clutched her stomach and laughed hard. When she recovered, she said, "That was you? That's hilarious. I didn't recognize you without the goat. I must admit, my eyes were on that goat the whole time. I've never seen anything so funny in all my life."

"We noticed the goat milk products on the wall," I said, gesturing to said products. "My twin sister is Amish, and her community is about to have a market to raise funds for an Amish widow's medical expenses. We were hoping you would make a donation, no matter how small."

"Yes, Digby explained that to me." Her eyes alighted on the cake on the desk. "What's that?"

"We brought him an Amish Bible Cake by way of apology," I said.

"That's very kind of you." She tut-tutted. "Imagine Digby leaving it here!" She crossed to the desk to pick it up. "Come and have a drink with me, won't you? We will share the cake. No point leaving it for Digby." She winked at us and beckoned us to follow her into the main part of the house.

Paisley indicated we should sit on large white couches. I figured there must be money in the goat milk product industry as the house was lavishly furnished in a Hamptons style. It looked lovely, even though we were nowhere near a beach.

Everything was white, with touches of washed out blue. There were natural fibers, timber floors, and expansive glass windows.

Classical music played softly in the background. A candle was burning on the coffee table in front of me. I bent forward to smell it. The scent was strongly lavender, although I detected subtle notes of something else, maybe jasmine.

"Lavender," Paisley supplied, somewhat unnecessarily. "It keeps me calm. What would you like to drink?"

"Would you have any herb tea?" I asked her.

"I have lemon and ginger."

"That would be perfect, thank you."

She looked expectedly at Matilda and Eleanor. "Do you have any hard liquor?" Eleanor asked her. "Brandy? Gin? Whiskey?"

Matilda kicked Eleanor in the shin. "My sister is joking. Coffee would be lovely for us both please, cream and one sugar."

Paisley looked confused but went into the kitchen. As it was an open concept house, we weren't able to whisper to each other, so I contented myself by looking around the room. There were also framed pictures of goats, but they were smaller ones propped up on furniture rather than hanging from walls.

When Paisley returned, she set our drinks along with the Amish Bible Cake on the coffee table. Matilda thanked her. "This is a beautiful house. Have you lived here for long?"

Paisley nodded. "We moved here soon after we were married, almost thirty years ago."

"You must have been married awfully young," Matilda said.

Paisley chuckled. Matilda's comment obviously pleased her.

"That's a long time to be married," Eleanor said. "I think if I had been married to a man that long, I would have murdered him."

I couldn't help but gasp. I quickly looked at Paisley. She too was shocked but soon covered her expression. "Well, I can't say I haven't thought about it from time to time," she said with a chuckle. "Digby can be irritating at times."

I wondered if she did know about his affair with Gemma or whether she simply suspected it. Or maybe she did know, and she had been the one who killed Gemma. I realized she was drinking brandy, given that she was drinking from a brandy balloon. Gemma had been killed by shots. I wondered if she had been doing shots with Paisley.

Paisley changed the subject. "We do produce gift baskets of the goat products," she said. "I'll just pop outside to our storage room and bring back one for you." She put down her drink and left by the French doors overlooking expansive lawns. I watched as she walked out to a small wooden building.

I opened my mouth to say something, but Matilda shook her head. I realized that we hadn't seen Digby since we had been in the living room and clearly, Matilda was afraid he would overhear if we said something. Instead, I said, "Isn't this a beautiful house!"

"Yes, it is indeed." Matilda stood up and walked over to a dresser against the wall and then walked back to her seat. Paisley wasn't away long. She returned with a big basket covered in clear cellophane wrap and sporting a huge purple big bow. "I can donate this," she said. "Will this do?"

"It absolutely perfect," I gushed. "Thank you so much. That's very kind of you."

"Not at all," she said. "You said your sister is Amish?"

I nodded. "My twin sister, Rebecca, has the Amish cupcake store in town."

"So, you were raised Amish?"

I nodded again. "Yes. I left the Amish after my *rumspringa*. I never rejoined the community."

Paisley nodded. "It was actually an Amish lady who got me involved with goats."

That got my interest. "Oh, really?"

She nodded again. "I can't remember her name. I was a child at the time and she had become friends with my mother. This wasn't in these parts, mind you—we lived in Ohio. She had a little milking goat, and she showed me how to milk goats. That's what got me interested in goats. I was actually showing a Saanen when I met Digby. He was already heavily into breeding Alpines, so I just kind of fell into breeding Alpines too."

"Ah yes, well, it's very kind of you to make the donation," I said. "I'm sure everyone in the goat community is shocked by Gemma Calhoun's death."

Before Paisley could say respond, Matilda added, "It was a lovely funeral service, wasn't it?"

"Yes, it was." Paisley's expression gave nothing away. "Gemma was very dedicated to her goats. I wonder if they'll ever find out who murdered her."

I thought that a strange thing to say. "I'm sure they'll find out sooner or later," I said. "The police generally do solve murder cases in the end."

She shook her head. "No, not always. I watch those unsolved crime shows on TV, and even if they think they know who it is, they often have trouble proving it."

"Yes, I like watching those shows too," Matilda said. "Who do you think murdered her?"

Paisley looked surprised. "I don't know."

"But you must have thought about it," Matilda pressed her. "People like us—that is, people who like those crime shows on TV—have analytical minds, don't we? I'm sure you have your suspicions."

Paisley seemed to be considering Matilda's words. After a brief silence, she said, "I wouldn't like to say anything bad about anybody, but I do suspect her son, Horatio. He and Gemma had a rocky relationship, and he inherits everything. And he wasted no time getting rid of her goats. I heard he sold them for a pittance. That would have upset Gemma. That's probably why he did it."

"Yes, it does seem suspicious," I said, "but why murder her at a goat show? Surely, he had plenty of opportunity to murder her somewhere else."

Paisley adjusted a blue and white cushion behind her back. "But then it would point suspicion to him if he murdered her at her home."

"Did you see Horatio at the goat show at all?" I asked her.

She shook her head. "No, but if he murdered Gemma, then he would have been hiding from everybody."

"Somebody needs to look into that man's alibi," Matilda said.

16

I had tossed and turned all night. I was still concerned about Rebecca leasing the apartment to Aaron Alexander, although Rebecca seemed entirely unconcerned.

I tiptoed down the stairs to the kitchen. I enjoyed the morning solitude with a fresh pot of steaming coffee, and the years of awaking before dawn when I was Amish had stayed with me. Now I didn't have the chores, but I still enjoyed that hour of the morning when everything was quiet. It seemed as though I was the only person awake in the whole world.

Alas, the peaceful solitude did not last long. Matilda burst through the door and slammed a newspaper in front of me, causing my coffee to jiggle. She jabbed her stubby finger on the paper. "Look at that!"

I took a sip of coffee before looking at the paper. *Baby born with six legs might be alien*, was the blaring headline. I was entirely confused. I looked up at Matilda. "What's this about?"

Matilda sighed and stabbed her finger on the paper again. I looked down at the photo. "It's obviously photoshopped," I said.

She planted her palm on her forehead. "Not the photo, Jane! Look at the name! The name of the journalist."

I looked at the paper, and then the penny dropped. "Horatio Calhoun-Blye!" I exclaimed. "He's a journalist!"

"I think that's giving him too much credit," she said, "but now we know he works for this newspaper. Obviously, the paper can't be taken seriously."

Eleanor walked into the room and sensibly headed straight for the coffee pot. "Yes, and it looks as though he has an alibi."

I was almost disappointed. "An alibi?" I repeated. "Are you sure?"

Matilda shook her head. She poured some coffee into a bowl and then broke some stale bread into the bowl. I had never gotten used to the idea of coffee soup, but Matilda seemed to enjoy it. "We can't be certain of anything," she said. "It's dangerous to be overconfident. That sort of thing can get you killed."

Eleanor sat opposite me and slipped her coffee noisily. "He was doing a story out of town, supposedly at the same time that

Gemma was murdered," she said. "That's what we are investigating today."

I got up and poured myself another coffee. After I sat down, I said, "Let me know what you find out."

The sisters exchanged glances. "What do you mean?" Matilda said. "You're coming with us."

"But I have to work," I said.

"But you said Rebecca is shutting the shop at midday today to get ready for tomorrow's fundraising market," Matilda countered. "Come on Jane, no more excuses. The three of us will investigate the suspect's alibi."

I knew when I was beaten. "Okay, but how *do* we investigate his alibi?"

"I've found the newspaper's YouTube channel." Eleanor spun her iPad around and showed me. A news reporter was standing by some fields pointing to road construction. She said the new road was going to bypass local businesses in a nearby town, and the businesses were all worried they'd lose their income. They had staged a protest.

When I finished watching, I looked up. "Well, there were no aliens thankfully, but I don't see what it has to do with Horatio."

"He's at twenty-five seconds," Eleanor said. After I shot her a look, she added, "You can see Horatio in the background at twenty-five seconds, directly behind the journalist."

I watched the video again. "Yes, it's definitely him for sure," I said, "but this footage could have been taken before his mother was murdered."

"That's what we have to find out," Matilda said. "We'll look into it some more and you can then collect us directly after you finish work."

"Where will we go?"

"That's precisely what we have to research. When you finish work, we'll be ready to go, and we'll tell you where we're going then."

I sighed. "Okay, but are you sure we can't leave this to Detective Stirling now? After all, he hasn't questioned you again."

"No, not yet." Matilda dropped her spoon into her bowl of coffee soup. "We can't afford for him to look too much into our backgrounds."

"Matilda!" Eleanor exclaimed.

"What backgrounds are those?" I asked her. I often wondered about their backgrounds, considering they were knowledgeable about all sorts of obscure matters and were even skilled in martial arts.

"Never you mind," Matilda said. "If we wanted everything about us to be known, then we would tell everybody. As it is, we need this murder solved, and the sooner the better."

I held up both hands in a gesture of defeat. "Okay. I'll collect you after work."

"And don't hang about," Matilda said. "Get back here as soon as you can."

The rest of the morning passed uneventfully. When we shut the shop, once more I waited for Rebecca to drive away in her buggy to make sure she wasn't left alone with Aaron Alexander, who was still high on my list of suspects.

I drove home, hoping I would have time to have a nice cup of hot meadow tea and put my feet up for a while, but Matilda and Eleanor were already waiting on the front porch for me. They hurried down the stairs to the car. "Let's go," Matilda said. Before I had a chance to ask where we were going, she told me. "We're going to that town that was in the newspaper."

"Did you find out anything else?" I asked them.

Matilda was the one who answered me. "We found out that Horatio has been working for that paper for some years now, and while it is a sensationalist newspaper, they sometimes do serious stories. His story on the road closure hasn't hit the paper yet."

"That's right," Eleanor said. "I actually called the paper. I pretended to be one of the storekeepers and asked when the story would be published, but the lady said she didn't know anything about it. She said I would have to wait until it came out."

"I also called the television station and asked them when it was filmed, and it was indeed filmed the very day that Gemma was murdered," Matilda told me.

"So how far away is this town exactly?"

"An hour and a half."

I gasped. "But that's a three-hour round trip! And I'm having dinner with Damon at six."

They both chuckled, and then Matilda added, "Then we had better not waste any time in that town. We'll just question people and leave. We can always go back another day if we need to follow up."

"So, what exactly do we need to find out?" I asked her.

"In the video, Horatio was standing next to a man," Matilda told me. "I did a reverse image search and found he owns a shoe store. We'll question him and see if Horatio interviewed him. Leave all the talking to us."

"But what if the store closes early today?" I asked her.

Eleanor, who was sitting in the passenger seat next to me, said, "No. They're staying open longer hours because they're worried about the road closure. It was all in that video you watched."

I was worried this was a wild goose chase, and I was also worried I wouldn't have enough time to go back and get ready for dinner with Damon.

I was also concerned that the shoe store man wouldn't want to speak with us.

When we arrived in town, I was surprised to see the stores were quite busy. "The publicity has obviously done them some good," I remarked.

Eleanor leaned across me and pointed. "Park over there. It's not far from there to the shoe shop."

I did as she asked. Fortunately for us, there were no customers in the shoe store. The man we had seen in the photo was there. His face lit up when he saw what he no doubt thought were three customers walking through the door.

Matilda spoke first. "Hello, Mr. Larkin?"

He nodded.

"I'm afraid we're not here to buy shoes. We're following up on an alibi. We're from the Birtwistle Detective Agency, and we're here to ask questions about the alibi of Mr. Horatio Calhoun-Blye."

"Oh yes, that man from the newspaper."

"So, he did interview you?"

The man nodded. "Yes, I already told the police that."

"Detective Stirling?"

The man nodded. "Yes, that was him. He gave me the third degree."

Matilda afforded him a warm smile. "We don't actually work with Detective Stirling," she said. "If you wouldn't mind going through things again with us, that would be a big help."

"Sure, I'll help while I don't have any customers." He looked pointedly at the door.

"So, you do remember Mr. Calhoun-Blye interviewing you for his newspaper?" Before the man had a chance to respond, Matilda added, "Do you remember the exact time he interviewed you?"

"Sure I do. It was exactly at eleven. I put a sign on my door saying I would be back at eleven, and he started questioning me at eleven, which worried me. I thought I might get back to the shop to find angry customers." He shrugged. "But when I got back, there was nobody here, so I could have spoken with him longer, after all."

"Thanks, you've been very helpful," Matilda said.

We walked out of the store and stood on the pavement. "Then Horatio definitely can't be the murderer, I suppose," Matilda said sadly. "That's an ironclad alibi if ever I've heard one."

"What if Horatio was in it with somebody else, somebody who looks like him?" I said.

Matilda said, "Give me your iPad, Eleanor!" Eleanor did as she asked, and Matilda disappeared back inside the store. She emerged a few moments later. "I showed Mr. Larkin one of the profile photos from Horatio's social media, and he is absolutely certain it was the same person. He even got Horatio's height right."

My spirits fell. "Then it wasn't him. Horatio was the one with the strongest motive. The funeral was rather lavish, though," I added. "If he murdered his mother, you wouldn't think he would spend so much on her funeral."

Matilda waved her finger at me. "To the contrary, that's exactly what a murderer would do, spend more money on their victim's funeral to throw the police off the track. Still, it can't have been him."

"Then who was it?" I said.

17

I was glad it wasn't raining for the market that day. Rain hadn't been forecast but then again, that didn't mean much. I sat in the kitchen and sipped my coffee. Only Mr. Crumbles was with me. I had given him his breakfast and he was now licking his paws.

"There you are, Jane," said Matilda's booming voice from the doorway.

"Where else would I be?" I said with a chuckle.

Matilda walked into the kitchen to make her breakfast. "Asleep in bed and snoring your head off like Eleanor. Couldn't you hear her? Or did I only hear her because there's a common wall?"

"I do not snore!" Eleanor yelled from the doorway.

"Coffee, Eleanor?" I said to stop the argument. "I'm glad it's not raining today."

"Yes, it would make the investigation so much more difficult."

I handed Eleanor a cup of coffee. "What do you mean?"

"Sloshing around in the rain, of course."

I sat down and took another gulp of coffee before continuing. "No, I mean how can we possibly investigate today? I doubt the suspects will even be there."

Eleanor fed Mr. Crumbles. "I've already fed him," I said.

"But he looked hungry," she protested.

I simply shrugged. Eleanor took a seat at the table. "Now let's see who we have as suspects. Our main suspect is Horatio, although he has an ironclad alibi."

"Perhaps he deliberately set up that alibi, and he was in it with the person who did the actual poisoning," I said.

Matilda nodded and tapped away on her phone.

"What on earth are you doing, Matilda?" Eleanor asked her.

"I'm emailing myself a reminder to look into his assignment," Matilda said. "Jane made a good point. But if Jane is right, then who could Horatio possibly be in partnership with?" She slurped her a coffee soup, causing Eleanor to grimace.

"Francis?" I offered with a shrug. "He did sell her the goats and cheaply at that."

"But she wouldn't have admitted that he sold them to her cheaply if she was his accomplice," Matilda said.

Eleanor sneezed, excused herself, and then said, "Why not?"

"Because it would throw suspicion onto her," Matilda said.

Eleanor shook her head. "I don't see why."

I walked over to the countertop to fetch the coffee pot. I poured myself another cup and looked out of the kitchen window. The first rays of sunlight were making their way over the horizon. I reflected on the fact this used to be my favorite time of day before Matilda and Eleanor decided to be such early risers. Maybe I should make coffee and take it back to my bedroom from now on. Then again, I figured Mr. Crumbles would seek me out and scratch on my door because he was used to getting his breakfast early, and if there is one thing a cat doesn't like, it's not being fed on time.

"Jane!"

I turned around. "Yes, Matilda?"

"I still haven't finished discussing the suspects."

I took my coffee to the table and sat down.

Eleanor yawned and stretched. "Who do we have? Horatio and Francis, and Cynthia, Gemma's best friend. It's strange she and Gemma had a falling out and then became friends again just before Gemma was murdered."

Matilda quirked one eyebrow. "You think they still had a falling out and Cynthia went there to murder her?"

"That's a possibility we need to consider," I said. "And Cynthia said it was over a man. Of course, she might have been lying."

"They're all lying, as far as we know." Matilda drummed two fingers on the table. "And then there's Digby Thompson and his wife, Paisley. We've heard that Gemma was having an affair with Digby. Maybe Cynthia was having an affair with Digby too, so she decided to murder Gemma to get her out of the way."

That didn't make sense to me and I said so. "Then wouldn't Cynthia murder Paisley instead of Gemma?"

Eleanor agreed. "Or she would murder Gemma *and* Paisley."

"Paisley might be the murderer," Matilda said. "She found out her husband was having an affair with Gemma, so decided to murder Gemma."

I spooned some more sugar into my coffee. I figured I needed it. "But why wouldn't Paisley murder her husband instead?"

Both Eleanor and Matilda shook their heads vigorously. "For some reason, women don't blame their husbands when they discover they're having affairs," Matilda pointed out. "They usually blame the other woman."

"When I found out *my* husband was having an affair, I blamed him," I said, "not his junior, ever-so-young bride-to-be, Cherri." I pulled a face.

Matilda waved her hand at me in dismissal. "Sure, but most women place the blame firmly at the feet of the other woman."

I thought back to all the TV shows I had seen. "Maybe you're right."

"I'm always right," Matilda said dismissively. "Now, those are the only suspects we have?"

She held up her hands and ticked them off one by one on her fingers. "Horatio, who has an alibi but might have been working with somebody else. Francis, who bought all the prize goats cheaply from Horatio. Digby Thompson, Gemma's alleged lover. Paisley, Digby's wife, who would also have a motive.

And Cynthia, whose motive we don't yet know, but that doesn't mean she didn't have the best one of all. Have I forgotten anybody?"

"Aaron Alexander!" I said so loudly that both women jumped. "We have forgotten him! He's gone under the radar. It might have been him, and he's renting the apartment from my sister. What if he's the murderer?" I trembled.

Matilda leaned forward and patted my hand. "Calm your farm, Jane. My instincts tell me he's not the murderer."

"When have your instincts ever been right, Matilda?" Eleanor said.

Matilda rounded on her furiously. "My instincts are always right!"

I interjected. "We had better get ready to go to the market."

"But it's too early." Matilda pointed out the window. "The sun has only just come up."

"We had better check the goats first. We want to make sure they haven't escaped from their field. Rebecca and Ephraim would be most unhappy if the goats got out."

"Yes, it would be nice to walk along and check the fence line," Matilda said.

Eleanor looked as though she strongly disagreed, but she wisely kept her opinions to herself.

Soon, the three of us were suitably dressed and walking to the goat's field. "They all look happy enough," Matilda said, "except Gigi is back to her normal dirty self. And I, for one, don't want to shampoo her again."

"You didn't shampoo her the first time," Eleanor said.

"I'm sure Gigi is much happier being left to her own devices," I said quickly. "I'm sure she doesn't want to be a show goat." To my relief, both sisters readily agreed.

"I'm still thinking about the shot glasses." Eleanor tapped her chin. "The murderer had to be somebody who Gemma would do shots with, such as a friend. You don't do shots with strangers."

"Still, that could be anybody. It doesn't rule anybody out."

I agreed with Matilda. "No wonder Detective Stirling hasn't solved the case yet. This is a hard one."

"He has access to more information than we do," Matilda said. "Did Damon give you any clues as to the status of the investigation?"

I felt my cheeks burn. "No, he didn't. Anyway, let's have breakfast and then go to the market."

"We've already had breakfast." Matilda looked me as though I had gone mad.

"I always have coffee very early and then I have a proper breakfast later," I said. "I haven't had my breakfast."

After breakfast, I drove to the markets. I was feeling restless and nervous about Aaron. Just because he loved animals didn't mean he wasn't a murderer. I had seen a documentary on TV where everybody thought a serial killer was a sweet man because he always rescued ants from puddles. It turned out he didn't feel the same way toward people. No, I was going to keep my eye firmly on Aaron.

The market was to be held in one of the parks on the edge of town. When we arrived, we saw row after row of Amish buggies.

"See, we're not early after all," Eleanor said.

Matilda chuckled. "Yes, we are. The Amish will always be here before anybody else."

Rebecca was already setting up her stall. I handed her the flask of coffee I'd brought for her. She thanked me. "Aaron has been a big help to me. He brought the cupcakes from the store in his car."

"Aaron!" I said, alarmed. "What's he done?"

"He helped bring all these cupcakes from the store for me this morning," she said. "I just said that."

"But I would have done that. Why didn't you ask me?"

"Because Aaron lives above the store." Rebecca looked up briefly while setting out the cupcakes.

I shot Matilda a pointed look. She nodded to show she had taken my meaning. "Is Aaron here now?" she asked Rebecca.

She dusted off her apron and looked around. "I don't know." She went back to her business.

"Let's look around and see if we can spot any of the suspects," Matilda suggested to me in little more than a whisper. "That will give us an opportunity to question them."

We had only gone a few steps when we all but bumped into Aaron who was rounding a corner. He did look genuinely pleased to see us.

"You don't have your cat with you." He almost sounded disappointed.

"No, I thought it might be too crowded for him," Eleanor said.

"I'm running another beginner class this afternoon. You should have had an email about it. Are you bringing him?"

Eleanor's hands flew to her head. "I had completely forgotten about that! Yes, of course, I'm bringing him."

We had all forgotten about the Pet Protection classes. That was a good opportunity to spend more time with Aaron to observe and to question him.

"That is, if the police don't want to question me again," Eleanor said, plastering a fake downcast look on her face for the benefit of Aaron. "Have they questioned you again?"

Aaron gave no indication that he found her question suspicious. "No, they haven't. Maybe they've caught whoever it is."

"Surely we would have heard if they had," I said.

He nodded slowly. "I hope they catch whoever did it. Gemma was really mean, but she didn't deserve to die." With that, he nodded before hurrying away.

I watched his departing back. "You know, he could have had any number of motives."

"Like what?" Eleanor asked me.

"Like, he said Gemma was mean. Maybe she had already given him notice and he pretended to us it was Horatio. Maybe she did treat him unfairly. Maybe she withheld his wages. Maybe she discovered a secret in his past and he had to do away with her before she told anybody."

"But that's all supposition," Matilda said.

"But we do need to consider it," Eleanor said. "The murderer had to be one of our suspects. And yet, we still don't know who it is."

18

Matilda, Eleanor, Mr. Crumbles, and I were once more at one of Aaron's Pet Protection training sessions. Matilda and I were sitting off to one side. I regarded all the large dogs with trepidation. They looked more like guard dogs than pets. Even though these were the same people who had been in the previous session, Aaron once more went through his long speech. I supposed it was necessary, but it wasn't necessary for me to hear it. I pulled out my phone and searched all the suspects' names once more and then searched Gemma's name.

Matilda noticed what I was doing and then did the same thing. After about five minutes, I looked up. Aaron was still speaking. The dogs had gone to sleep and so, I assume, had most of their owners. Eleanor was listening with rapt attention and was holding Mr. Crumbles. As I watched, he tried to get away several times, so she gave him treats.

"I'm sure this is a complete waste of time," Matilda said, stifling a yawn.

I too yawned and stretched. "There's no point attending these classes. We won't find out anything more about Aaron by coming here. And I'm still worried about him renting Rebecca's apartment."

Matilda nodded. "I know you are. Cookie?" She reached into her purse and pulled out some cookies.

"Thanks." I took one and chewed it too quickly. It tickled my throat, so I coughed. Matilda jumped to her feet and banged me on my back despite my protests.

"I'm all right," I said when I managed to find my voice. "You know, this murder has got me stumped. Horatio had the most obvious motive, but he has an alibi."

"Yes, he inherited everything, and her life insurance went to him too."

"Life insurance!" I shrieked. "Why didn't you tell me she had life insurance?"

"I assumed you knew. It will make Horatio a millionaire."

"Even *more* of a millionaire," I corrected her. "Just her house and her assets alone would surely be worth more than a million."

"That's a few million good reasons to murder somebody." Matilda smiled and nodded as she spoke.

"But Horatio has an undeniable alibi," I said. "Matilda, we need to check up on that. I know we mentioned it before, but we really need to go to the newspaper and find out the circumstances."

"What do you mean?"

I shrugged. "I don't know. It could give us some information we haven't uncovered yet."

Matilda patted my knee. "You're getting better at this, Jane. I should have thought of that myself."

I looked back up at the class. Aaron was making them do basic obedience training again. Every time a dog got close to Mr. Crumbles, he lashed out with one paw. Soon, all the dogs were giving him a wide berth.

"You know, cats would have been good in sieges," Matilda said.

I had no idea what she meant, so I asked for clarification.

"Well, when the besieged people ran out of boiling oil, they could have dropped cats on people's faces, of course," Matilda said. "Imagine a vicious cat landing on your face! You certainly wouldn't want to continue storming a fortress then."

I had to laugh. "Maybe Aaron should do specific cat attack training sessions."

I thought Matilda would laugh too, but she said, "You know, I think that's a great idea! I must bring that up with him at dinner tonight."

"Dinner tonight? Whatever are you talking about? Did you invite him to have dinner with us tonight?"

"Of course not. Rebecca has invited us all."

"And Aaron?"

She nodded. "And don't frown like that, Jane. It will give you even more wrinkles. It's a good opportunity to get more information out of him."

"What if he's the murderer? A murderer, renting the apartment from Rebecca?"

Matilda waved her finger at me. "All the more reason why we need to solve this quickly. Detective Stirling hasn't solved it yet, has he!"

"I suppose so," I said.

And so, hours later, I found myself sitting in Rebecca's living room, sipping meadow tea and waiting for Aaron to arrive. Matilda and Eleanor were helping Rebecca in the kitchen and had left me to wait for Aaron. I could have done both, but they had insisted. Rebecca's husband, Ephraim, was not to arrive for another hour or so.

Finally, there was a loud knock on the door, and I crossed to open it. I paused halfway, suddenly afraid it would be Detective Stirling wanting to question us further. I was relieved a little when I opened the door and saw it was Aaron. I plastered a fake smile on my face. "Come in, won't you."

He came inside and looked around. "I've never been in an Amish house before," he said. I could see he was doing his best not to stare. Not that there was much to stare at in an Amish home—there wasn't exactly an overabundance of furniture or decoration in such houses.

The floors were timber. The couches were plain, although one did have a Star of Bethlehem quilt that Rebecca had made over it. Plain blue curtains hung from the windows. There was a large wooden clock on the wall. A beige, short-pile floor rug sat under the coffee table between the two couches. Noticeably absent was the hum of electricity.

Rebecca, Matilda, and Eleanor walked in. "*Hiya*, Aaron," Rebecca said. "Have you had meadow tea before?"

"No, I haven't," he said. "What does it taste like?"

"Peppermint," I said as Rebecca handed him a cup. He looked doubtful, but after he sipped some, his face relaxed. "It's actually quite nice, and I don't like herbal tea. This is quite strong though. I like it."

"Well, I'll just see to the dinner," Rebecca said and then vanished. This time Matilda and Eleanor sat with me on the couch.

"I'm a little bit nervous," Aaron said in hushed tones. "What do I have to do so as not to offend Rebecca and her husband?"

"Obviously, you mustn't swear or blaspheme or take the Lord's name in vain," Matilda said.

"And before and after the meal there is a silent prayer," I told him. "Just follow Ephraim's lead. Before anyone eats, we will all close our eyes, and then we open our eyes a minute or so later."

Aaron appeared alarmed. "How will I know when to open my eyes?"

"I'll kick you under the table if I can reach," Eleanor said cheerfully.

Aaron looked even more alarmed.

"Recite the Lord's Prayer silently," I told him. "That's usually about the time it takes. And if you don't open your eyes by the time everybody else has, Eleanor can clear her throat to signal you."

Aaron shot Eleanor a grateful look. "Is that all I need to know?"

I nodded. "You'll be all right."

Matilda piped up. "Aaron, I've been meaning to ask you. Jane and I discussed this while we were watching your class today, and I wondered if you should have Pet Protection classes just for cats."

Aaron's hand flew to his throat. He looked even more shocked now. "Cats!" he said in horror.

Matilda pushed on. "Yes, Mr. Crumbles is doing well in your class."

Aaron grimaced. "Mr. Crumbles is a most unusual cat, and we haven't started defense classes yet."

"By defense, I assume you mean attack," Eleanor said. "I will have you know, Mr. Crumbles has already saved Jane's life on three separate occasions."

"You already told me about that—at some length." Aaron wiped his hand over his brow. "I doubt I could train a cat to do what Mr. Crumbles did. It must come naturally to him." He pulled a face.

Eleanor narrowed her eyes, but Matilda seemed unconcerned. "Yes, I was telling Jane that cats would be good in a siege situation."

I actually felt sorry for Aaron. His jaw fell open. It took him a moment or two to recover. "A siege situation?" he repeated. His eyes darted from side to side.

Matilda nodded. "Imagine if you were in a fortress and people were climbing up your walls and you had run out of boiling oil to pour on them. You could drop cats on their faces."

A sudden urge to laugh overwhelmed me. I clutched my stomach and hurried out of the room. When I got to the kitchen, I sucked in deep breaths.

"Is something the matter?" Rebecca asked me, searching my face.

"Matilda," I said, when I figured I could speak without laughing hysterically. "She has poor Aaron cornered and she's suggesting that people in siege situations should drop cats on people's faces."

Rebecca did not appear interested in the least. "Here, Jane. Could you put this on the table for me?" She handed me a large loaf of homemade bread.

I took it from her and walked back out. Aaron was busy explaining to Matilda that people don't storm fortresses these days.

Matilda seemed quite put out. "Obviously, I know that. It's the principal, don't you see?"

"Oh yes, I see," Aaron muttered, although it was clear that he didn't.

The door opened, and Ephraim strode in. "Nice to see you all again," he said. "*Hullo*, Aaron."

Aaron jumped up and shook his hand.

"I was able to get home sooner than I expected," Ephraim said. "*Hiya* Jane, Matilda, and Eleanor. *Wie gehts?*"

"We're *gut, denki*," Eleanor said with a smirk at Matilda.

Rebecca walked out. "Ephraim! You're home early." She beamed from ear to ear.

"I was just going back to the kitchen to help you," I said.

Soon we were all sitting around the table. Aaron came through the silent prayer unscathed, even though after Eleanor had cleared her throat, he had yelped and said 'Ouch!' Given that she was sitting opposite him, I suppose she had delivered a kick to his shins.

The table was laden with pickled beets, chow chow relish, schnitz und knepp, and a layered lettuce salad. The dessert, Amish Funny Cake Pie, was sitting there too and would later be joined by vanilla ice cream.

"You're such a good cook, Rebecca," Aaron said. "You've been so kind to me, leasing me the apartment with me being a complete stranger."

"I expect most people lease apartments to complete strangers," Rebecca said with a laugh.

Aaron laughed too. Everybody else at the table seemed relaxed, but I was still concerned that he was the murderer. I wondered how I could bring the subject around to Gemma's death and was still wondering when Matilda did it for me.

"Has Detective Stirling questioned you again?" she asked him rather pointedly.

"Yes, as a matter of fact, the detective questioned me yesterday. Has he questioned you again?"

Matilda pulled a face. "Thankfully, he hasn't. Did you get any clue from him as to whether he was close to solving the case?"

Aaron shook his head. "No, he just asked a lot of questions about Horatio."

"Horatio? Doesn't he have an alibi?"

"I don't know. Detective Stirling didn't ask me any questions about Horatio's alibi."

"What sort of questions did he ask you?" Matilda pressed.

"Just about Horatio's love life, not that I knew anything about that," Aaron said with a chuckle. "I'd heard rumors about Gemma's love life, of course, but not about Horatio's. All I knew was that Gemma had threatened to cut him out of her will."

I gasped. "Why would she do that?"

"Like I told the detective, Gemma wasn't able to control her temper at the best of times. When I was milking the goats one day, she came in and yelled that she was about to change her will because she didn't like Horatio's taste in women."

"Was that just before she was murdered?" Matilda asked him.

Aaron shook his head. "No, it was a few months ago."

"I might have to start the fire," Ephraim said, cutting across the conversation. "The nights are getting cooler earlier this year, don't you think so, Aaron?"

"I hadn't quite noticed, to tell you the truth, because I've always had air-conditioning," Aaron said. "But yes, I see what you mean. It must be good to be closer to nature and therefore more observant."

I knew Ephraim had changed the topic away from murder, as he didn't consider murder a suitable subject for dinner conversation. Still, I found it interesting. I hadn't heard previously that Gemma had threatened to cut Horatio out of her will.

Something niggled at me at the back of my mind. Obviously, Gemma hadn't changed her will because Horatio was to inherit everything, so maybe he had dumped his girlfriend—or simply had pretended to do so. And if that had been the case, had Horatio plotted to murder his mother from that moment forward? It would certainly make sense, but just because the pieces fitted didn't mean they were the right pieces.

And there was something else, that something niggling at me at the back of my mind. It was one of those things I knew that I couldn't quite bring forward to full realization. It was entirely irritating, but the more I thought about it, the more it eluded me.

Aaron nodded to the seat opposite him. "Is that an Amish custom?"

"Is what?" Rebecca asked him.

"Setting a spare place for dinner," he said. "I've heard you Amish are very hospitable. Is that because somebody could drop by with no warning?"

Both Ephraim and Rebecca chuckled. I hadn't even noticed the extra place until he mentioned it, so consumed I was with my concerns that Aaron might be the murderer.

"No, we invited somebody else as a surprise, but he didn't know if he could make it," Rebecca said.

"Who was that?" Aaron asked.

Just then, there was a knock on the door. Ephraim stood. "That must be him now." He presently returned with Damon.

"Damon!" I gasped. My cheeks burned hot and I realized they were likely bright red. That made me embarrassed, which no doubt turned my cheeks a deeper shade of red.

Damon shot me a warm smile. "Hi, Jane. Hello, everybody. Thanks for inviting me, Rebecca."

"Aaron, you wouldn't have met Damon," Ephraim said. "Damon, this is Aaron

Alexander, our new tenant in the apartment. Aaron, this is Detective Damon McCloud."

"We actually met at a recent funeral," Damon said.

Aaron gasped. "A detective!" He sounded horrified but soon added, "I had better be on my best behavior." He forced a chuckle. "I didn't know Amish people had detectives for friends."

"Damon is Jane's friend," Ephraim said which made me blush furiously. I silently scolded myself.

"You have met my partner, Detective Stirling, I believe," Damon said.

Aaron's mouth fell open. "You're his partner? So, are you working on Gemma Calhoun's murder?"

Damon shook his head. "No, I'm working on other cases at the moment. That is Detective Stirling's case."

"Does he have any suspects?" Aaron asked.

"You'd have to ask him," Damon said.

"I'm sorry, but we were all about to start," she said. "Please have a seat here right by me." The spare place was diagonally opposite me at the other end of the table, which is why I hadn't noticed it at first. I wished he had been seated closer.

After Damon was seated, Ephraim and Rebecca shut their eyes for the second silent prayer, which no doubt, was for Damon's benefit. The rest of us followed suit. I opened one eye to see Aaron had his eyes shut too.

I silently recited the Lord's Prayer to myself and then opened my eyes just as Rebecca and Ephraim opened theirs. Presently, there was another 'Ouch!' from Aaron. He bent down to rub his shin. "I know how long it takes now," he said to Eleanor in a pained tone.

Rebecca cleared her throat. "Help yourselves, everybody."

Soon I had a large helping of *schnitz und knepp* in front of me. I felt better knowing that Damon was there. If Aaron was, in fact, the murderer, then maybe he would be too scared to do anything as now he knew we were friends with Damon. I certainly hoped so, anyway.

Rebecca and Ephraim were careful to keep the conversation away from murder for the remainder of the dinner.

By the time we were all eating dessert, Amish Funny Cake Pie with ice cream, everybody appeared relaxed, even Aaron. I wondered if a murderer would be so calm in the presence of a detective. I had no idea. I wasn't a psychiatrist, and I couldn't help but worry.

Matilda, Eleanor, and I helped Rebecca clear the dinner table. When we returned, Rebecca asked, "Would everybody like *kaffi* or meadow tea?"

"I'll have what everybody else is having," Aaron said.

"That's most accommodating of you," Rebecca said with a smile, "but some will be having *kaffi* and some will be having meadow tea."

"*Kaffi* is coffee," Eleanor told him.

Aaron chuckled. "I figured that out for myself. I'd like some coffee please. Black."

Damon jumped to his feet. "I'll help you make the coffee and meadow tea."

"*Nee*," Rebecca said. She did her best to wave him away.

"I'll get it, and Damon can help me," I said with a pointed look at Rebecca.

She caught my meaning. "All right."

Damon and I walked into the kitchen. "Damon, I'm so happy you're here! It will make Aaron a little more scared to do anything, if he's the murderer."

Damon pulled me into a tight hug and whispered in my ear, "When you said you were happy I was here, I thought you were pleased to see me."

I chuckled. "I *am* pleased to see you. I just can't help worrying that Aaron is the murderer."

Damon released me. "That's why I wanted to catch you on your own."

"Oh, is that the only reason?" I teased him.

He wagged his finger at me. "Touché! I wanted to give you some information. I'm only telling you, mind you, because I think it will put your mind at rest about Aaron."

"You don't think he's the murderer?" I said a little too loudly and then clamped my hand over my mouth.

"Gemma Calhoun had an appointment with her lawyer to change her will."

"You're kidding!"

He shook his head. "The appointment was set for a few days after she was murdered. She told her lawyer that she was cutting Horatio out of the will because she didn't like his taste in women and he had been warned."

"So Horatio was still with the woman Gemma didn't like."

Damon folded his arms over his chest. "What do you know about that?"

"I'm sure I don't know anything that Detective Stirling doesn't know," I said. "I've just been concerned about Aaron living over Rebecca's store, in case he was the murderer and all that. This tends to implicate Horatio and his girlfriend, doesn't it?"

"I can't tell you anything, obviously, about an ongoing investigation," Damon said, "but I wouldn't worry about Aaron too much if I were you. Still, until we know for sure, don't take any chances, but I don't think you need to worry about him. The case has taken a different direction."

I reached up and gave him an impulsive peck on the cheek. "Thank you."

"Is that the best you can do?" Damon pulled me to him, but when his lips were inches away from mine, Eleanor burst through the door. "What's the delay? Some of us are desperate for coffee."

19

It had been an uneventful day. Matilda had done her best to try to convince me to break into Horatio's house, but I had flatly refused.

Now, I fixed my hair in the mirror. I wore a white Dior suit, one taken—with permission —from the back of Matilda's closet. The suit was too big on me, but that was nothing a couple of strategically placed pins couldn't conquer.

"You look lovely," Eleanor said as I descended the stairs. I felt like the heroine in one of those romantic comedies which were popular during the nineties, the ones made for teenagers.

"Thank you. Is Damon here yet?"

"I want him to try my tomato mint tea." Eleanor pointed to a mug she had set on the entrance table. "It's like soup in a cup!"

"It's nothing like soup in a cup," I said, distressed. I hardly wanted my first real date with Damon to begin with disaster, but if I didn't make a quick escape from my house mates, disaster was the only way I could see the night starting.

"The mint adds a touch of class," Eleanor said, ignoring me. "A touch of class, Jane! As if soup in a cup wasn't delightful enough already, it is *elegant* soup in a cup."

"Why don't you—I don't know—actually just put soup in a cup, Eleanor?"

"Now you are just talking nonsense, dear."

"You look beautiful, Jane," Matilda said kindly as she stepped into the entranceway. "Have either of you seen Gigi?"

I raised an eyebrow. "The goat?"

"Of course the goat," Matilda said. "She's gone, and she's such a wild little thing."

"I might have left the gate open," Eleanor said suddenly, and she clapped her hand over her mouth. "Get a flashlight, girls. We have an escapee."

"I don't have time," I replied. I didn't want to get the white suit dirty by running through the countryside at night, looking for a wild goat. "Is that Damon?"

The three of us listened as a car pulled into the driveway.

"He can help!" Eleanor exclaimed.

"Four hands are better than three!" Matilda agreed.

I threw open the door and darted toward the car. Damon had one foot on the ground, when he spotted me barreling forward, insisting that we needed to leave now. "Is anything wrong?"

"*Everything* is wrong," I called.

I could feel Eleanor and Matilda hot on my heels, their breathing heavy in the raw night air.

"They have tea that is like soup in a cup," I warned Damon.

"And a missing goat," Matilda added.

"No," I hissed as Damon opened his mouth to reply. I pushed him toward his door and then threw myself into the passenger seat, punching the lock and snapping on my seatbelt.

Eleanor and Matilda pressed their faces against the window, fogging up the glass. They looked like zombies.

"Help us," they moaned together. "Help us find Gigi."

"Drive," I urged Damon, who started the car, hit the gas, and tore away from the farmhouse.

"Did you hear that?" Damon said. "It sounded like something fell on the roof. We should stop and check."

But I had frightful visions of Eleanor and Matilda running toward us, arms filled with tomatoes and mint. "Keep driving," I ordered, surprised by the authority in my voice. Who knew I was so bossy!

The restaurant was a twenty-minute drive, and we arrived just in time to make our reservation. I believed that Damon had played the law enforcement card, because I'd heard people had tried to eat here for years at this fancy French restaurant and could never get a table.

Damon asked me to stay in the car because he wanted to open the car door for me. I found myself frowning as my phone chirped again and again with frantic texts from Eleanor and Matilda.

"Did you hear that?" Damon said, resting his hand on the door handle. He had not stepped from the car yet. "I thought I heard something on the roof."

"I didn't hear a thing," I said, but there it was. The sound of hooves on the roof of his car.

I didn't wait for Damon. I threw open my door and looked up, staring straight into the big yellow eyes of Gigi. So when Damon said he heard something on the roof, he was talking about the escaped goat!

"Oh no," I said to Gigi. "I've been looking forward to this date for a long time."

"We'll just take her back," Damon said calmly. He looked in the trunk for some rope.

"The restaurant will never hold our reservation. It'll take us forty minutes to drive home, return Gigi, and drive back here."

Damon tied the rope around Gigi's neck. "Eleanor and Matilda can come and collect her."

"It will take them twenty minutes to drive here," I replied, but Damon was already calling them.

I stood there and listened in on their conversation. So did Gigi, who was still on the roof. Damon told Eleanor and Matilda where we were. After he hung up, he said, "All good. They'll be here in twenty minutes."

"I don't think the restaurant will hold our table for twenty whole minutes, Damon." I didn't mean to sound so negative, but I'd heard this place was notorious for punishing latecomers. They could afford to be. They were the hot ticket in town.

"Why don't you go inside and hold our table, while I stay out here with Gigi to make sure she doesn't run away?"

I felt even guiltier now. Had I been so uptight about the reservation that Damon no longer wanted to eat dinner with me? These were the kind of thoughts that had haunted me in my youth, when I had felt so awkward and gawky on a date.

"Maybe I've overreacted."

"You've not overreacted at all." Damon took the end of the rope from me. "I'm not at all keen to lose this table either, not after Matilda and Eleanor told me this was your favorite restaurant."

I did a double take. "They did?" What were Matilda and Eleanor playing at? I kept my thoughts to myself. Clearly, Matilda and Eleanor wanted me at this restaurant for a reason, something to do with the investigation.

Damon was still talking. "I had to blackmail the sous-chef in order to get this reservation," he said with a wink.

I smiled. "Is that legal?"

"Of course not," Damon replied. "But it's smart. A man will go to great lengths to impress a pretty girl, you know."

I felt my ears redden. "Well, I'll just order a bottle of sparkling water and wait for you inside," I said, and he grinned.

For a moment, it felt as though we were the only two people in the world, until another car pulled into the parking lot, and the feeling was broken.

Damon stayed with Gigi as I took my seat in the restaurant. I ordered a soda along with a bottle of sparkling water and resisted the urge to reach for my phone. Plenty of grown women dined by themselves, so why should I feel embarrassed that no one was sitting across the table from me? Yet I did feel embarrassed. I felt as though the eyes of everyone in the restaurant were falling on me.

The feeling fled the minute Damon finally appeared at my elbow. "All good," he said, bending down, his breath brushing past my ear. "Matilda and Eleanor have taken Gigi. The taxi driver refused to take a goat in the car, so they borrowed my car to take her home. We'll catch a taxi back to your house." He smiled and sat opposite me.

I knew he wouldn't be smiling if he knew what Matilda's driving was like. Still, it was better that he remained oblivious to that.

A waiter appeared at our table and thrust menus at us. My eyes widened when I saw the prices. I was deciding between the Creamy Crab Croquettes with Wasabi Aioli and the Roasted Chicken Stuffed with Thyme and Truffle Oil, when the reason Matilda and Eleanor had seen to it that I came to this restaurant walked past me.

It was the elusive Horatio. I gasped.

Damon looked up at me. "Are you all right?"

I hesitated. I didn't want to start a relationship with lies, but he would be angry if his suspicions that I was investigating were confirmed. I considered for a moment telling him I was excited to see Asparagus in a Port Wine Gastrique on the menu, but honesty prevailed. "Horatio Calhoun-Blye just walked past us."

Damon raised one eyebrow. "The victim's son." Damon picked up his napkin, folded it, unfolded it, and put it back on his lap. "So, this isn't your favorite restaurant, is it?"

I had to admit that it wasn't. I hurried to add, "But it *is* a lovely restaurant, and I'm certain it *will* be my favorite restaurant going forward. I do love French food. Damon, I had no idea Matilda and Eleanor suggested you bring me here. I was puzzled, right until I saw Horatio."

Damon nodded. "I expect Horatio comes here all the time, and the sisters wanted you here to spy on him."

I shook my head. "I had no idea."

Damon sighed. He reached out and laid his hand on mine, sending little electric tingles running through me. "I know you didn't, Jane, but I haven't brought my work to dinner. Can we have a suspect-free dinner?"

"That's what I want!" I protested, a little too loudly. "I had no idea Matilda and Eleanor did this." *And wait until I give them a piece of my mind!* I added silently.

Still, I couldn't help thinking about Horatio. He was here alone. His mother had been about to cut him out of her will over her disapproval of his relationship with the mystery woman. Now that Gemma was dead, there was no reason for Horatio not to appear in public with his girlfriend—that is, unless they were joint murderers and thought a public appearance would tip off the police.

I thought about it some more, and figured Horatio wouldn't want his girlfriend's identity to be public knowledge anyway. Before I left the restaurant, I would have to ask somebody if Horatio had been seen here with a woman on a regular basis. Maybe I would be able to get a description.

My opportunity came moments later. Damon's phone rang. He spoke into it briefly, looked at me, said, "Sorry, Jane. This is urgent," before taking the phone outside.

I beckoned to the waiter. "Are those private dining rooms through there?" I nodded my head in the direction I had seen Horatio.

The waiter nodded. I pushed on.

"I thought I saw the son of a friend of mine go in there, but I don't want to disturb him. Horatio Calhoun-Blye?"

The waiter nodded. "Mr. Calhoun-Blye comes here all the time."

"With his girlfriend?"

The waiter nodded again.

"I forget her name."

The waiter simply looked at me.

"I forget her name," I said, more loudly this time. "What does she look like?"

The waiter frowned. "A woman of middle age."

"Blonde or brown hair?"

"I'm sorry, madam, I haven't really taken any notice. Light brown, I think." With that, he afforded me a small nod before hurrying away.

That didn't help. Francis's hair was light brown, whereas Cynthia's hair was dark blonde. They were both about the same height and build. Or maybe it was somebody else. Paisley? Her hair was light blonde. Yet if Horatio and his mystery girlfriend were planning to murder somebody, surely his girlfriend would wear a wig out in public, even if dining in a private room.

Damon's face was downcast when he returned to our table. "I'm afraid there's been a development in my case. Despite what I said about not wanting to bring my work to dinner, I have to go."

I was certain disappointment was stamped all over my face. Damon led me outside, where he helped me put on my coat. "I'll take you home."

I protested, but Damon wouldn't take no for an answer. He sat in the back of the taxi with me, and we giggled as if we were a pair of naughty school children. The driver did his best to ignore us, but he ended up putting on the radio and singing off-key.

"Thank you for, um, the attempt at dinner," I said as Damon walked me to the door. His car sat in the driveway, waiting to spirit him away. "It was lovely."

"Liar," he said, and we both started giggling again.

Suddenly, he stepped forward and brushed a lock of hair out of my eyes. "Jane..."

"Yes?"

He leaned forward, his lips hovering above mine. He smelled warm, and he smelled soft, like fresh laundry. I knew he was about to kiss me. I tried to steady the thudding of my heart, but it was no use. My legs were spaghetti now, even my arms felt limp. We were so close—so close!—but then Eleanor burst from the house.

"Quick! It's Matilda! There's been a terrible emergency."

Damon and I darted into the house. And there she was, Matilda, standing there, clutching her head.

"What happened?" I asked.

She turned around. The hair on the back of her head was missing. Had Eleanor decided to try her hand at hair styling? It was all too confusing.

"Gigi," Matilda said angrily when she saw our shocked faces. "Gigi ate my hair in the car."

I caught my breath. "It doesn't look like a mullet at all," I said.

"Who said it looked like a mullet?" Matilda's mouth dropped open.

Oops. I almost turned to Damon and asked if I could flee in his car with him, but the dastardly man said goodbye and strode from the house, leaving me with Eleanor, Matilda, and Matilda's mullet.

"I mean, it worked for Billy Ray Cyrus," I said desperately, searching for a way to soothe the situation.

"Go away!" Matilda sputtered.

She didn't have to tell me twice. I hurried out of the room, wondering if I should have said Mel Gibson instead.

20

The newspaper office exterior was unassuming, just a glass door in a brick wall. The entrance was equally unimpressive, a small room with a flight of stairs directly ahead. To the left appeared to be an empty room, and to the right was a frosted glass door with 'Office' stamped across it in tiny black lettering. Matilda slid it across and we walked in.

A young woman approached us. "Are you here about advertising?"

"No," Matilda said. "We're here to see Horatio Calhoun-Blye."

The young woman frowned. "He left about fifteen minutes or so ago." Of course, we knew this as Eleanor had called the newspaper's editor and insisted Horatio meet her out of town under the pretense she would show him several clear photographs of a UFO sighting. She had told the editor she refused to speak with anyone but Horatio.

"That's most distressing," Matilda said. "I was a good friend of his mother's. Horatio said we could meet for lunch today. Maybe he got an assignment and left the building in a hurry."

"Would you like to leave him a message?"

Matilda waved one hand at her. "That's okay. I'll text him. He never picks up when I call. I suppose there's no point waiting for him?"

The woman shook her head. "I'm afraid not. He could be gone for hours."

"He told me your paper wasn't investigating his mother's murder," Matilda said.

"No, it isn't that type of a newspaper here," the woman said with a chuckle. She lowered her voice and added, "It's more of a sensationalist newspaper, if you get my meaning."

We all nodded. Matilda pushed on. "But the day his mother died, Horatio was covering rather a serious story, wasn't he? I thought that was a rather unusual type of story for your paper."

The woman readily agreed. "Horatio insisted on covering it."

Matilda looked back over her shoulder and shot us a glance. To the woman, she said, "Did he say why? I did ask him, but he never makes much sense. The young people of today!"

"He said he wanted to do something serious for once. He insisted. The editor wasn't too thrilled about it, but Horatio has been here for so long that he gave him some leeway, I expect. It's such a small newspaper that we have to double up with jobs. I sell advertising, both classifieds and feature advertising, and I also do admin. Sometimes, they even make me write some stories—minor ones, of course," she added. "It's not a very big newspaper."

"Still, it's a very interesting one," Matilda offered with a wide smile.

"Yes, it is."

"Well, I was hoping to catch up with Horatio while I was in town, but I don't think I have time to wait for him. I was hoping to cheer him up."

"Cheer him up? Oh yes, after his mother's death. It's so terrible."

"Yes it is, and poor Horatio has been upset for a few months now ever since his mother made him give up his girlfriend."

"That's what *she* thought." The woman chuckled.

Eleanor stepped forward. "What do you mean?"

"I'm certain Horatio didn't give up his girlfriend. He was always making private calls."

"Maybe he got himself a new girlfriend," Matilda said.

She shook her head. "No, nothing ever changed with Horatio. His mother actually came in here once and demanded to know if we'd seen his girlfriend lately."

"Had you ever met his girlfriend?" I asked her.

She shook her head. "No. He never brought her here."

"So you don't know her name?"

"No, I wouldn't have a clue. Look, I've probably said too much."

"Well then, I won't tell Horatio I've even spoken to you," Matilda said. "Maybe I should simply call him and say I'm running late and that I'll arrange a meeting at another time."

We all smiled and left the building. "I need coffee and cake after that big disclosure," I said. "Look, there's a little café there."

The café had a narrow shop front, but when we walked inside, I saw the building continued a considerable distance. We took seats down the back, away from other patrons.

"My money is on Horatio," Matilda said. "I was so shocked when she said he insisted on that assignment. Obviously, he put a lot of work into his alibi."

I opened my mouth to agree with her, but a waitress walked up. We all ordered coffee but spent more time figuring out the food we wanted. Eleanor couldn't decide between a Bacon and Egg Bagel or a Triple Berry Cake, and Matilda couldn't decide between a Ham and Brie Panini or a Banana Chocolate Chip Buttercream cake. In the end, they opted for both. I wasn't so fussy. I simply craved fat and sugar, so I selected the Grilled French Toast with maple syrup and stuffed with sweet cream cheese.

When the waitress left, I said, "So then, it seems as though Horatio was the murderer, and he was in it with his girlfriend. Obviously, he didn't break up with his girlfriend months ago like his mother thought he did at the time. The question is, who is his girlfriend?"

"Let's examine what we know about the girlfriend," Matilda said. "Firstly, Gemma deemed her unsuitable. Secondly, she was at the goat show and was obviously doing shots with Gemma, so Gemma must have thought the girlfriend's relationship with Horatio was well and truly over."

I disagreed. "Why then would Gemma have made the appointment with her lawyer to change the will?"

Both Matilda and Eleanor frowned.

"You know, I can think of two people who might be the girlfriend," I said. "Cynthia was at the goat show and had the opportunity. The same can be said for Francis. I don't know where Cynthia was at the time Gemma was murdered, but Francis wasn't around the goat ring or near her goat. She said she had to go to the bathroom, and the bathroom was near Gemma's office. She could have easily slipped in and pretended she was doing shots with Gemma."

Eleanor leaned across the table. "And both Francis and Cynthia are much older than Horatio. In fact, they are both about Gemma's age, so she would definitely have been opposed to him dating a much older woman."

"Yes, it could be either of them," Matilda said. "However, we don't know for certain that Horatio was involved in Gemma's murder. It could have been Digby or Paisley."

"That fact that Gemma threatened to cut Horatio out of the will doesn't mean he's the murderer," I pointed out.

Matilda wagged her finger at me. "Trust me, only guilty people have alibis."

Eleanor nodded knowingly. "That's right. It's highly suspicious that Horatio insisted upon that assignment which had him out of town at the very time his mother was murdered. It's all too convenient, if you ask me. What if he was having an affair with Paisley? His mother would certainly have disapproved of that."

"Or maybe it was simply a woman his own age, and Gemma didn't like her for some other reason," I said. "Everybody said Gemma was a thoroughly unpleasant person. Maybe she was just one of those mothers who didn't like her son's girlfriends, period."

Matilda and Eleanor agreed.

"One thing we haven't looked into is where to get coolant," Eleanor said.

"Obviously, because it's freely available anywhere," Matilda said. "It comes in a variety of colors and strengths. Some of them have safety levels of ethylene, so the murderer obviously didn't select one of those. Most of them have bittering agents to avoid poisoning by accident. Anybody can go and buy coolant."

Eleanor looked quite put out.

"I think we have come to a dead end here," I admitted. "Detective Stirling probably has the same information we do. He hasn't managed to solve the case, and he's a professional."

"So am I," Eleanor said.

I fixed her with a steely look. "Excuse me?"

"Yes, explain yourself," Matilda said through gritted teeth. She folded her arms.

"I mean, we are just as clever as he is." Eleanor pretended to fumble through her purse.

I knew there was something strange about their pasts, and I wondered if I would ever find out what it was.

21

We all piled into my car. "I'll take you two home, and then I'll go back go to the shop." I checked my watch. "I feel bad leaving Rebecca on her own, especially with Aaron around." I knew Damon didn't think he was the murderer. That afforded me some small comfort, but I wasn't going to take any chances.

"No, take us to the shop and we will help Rebecca," Matilda insisted. "You go home and have a good sleep. You've been working too hard lately, Jane."

I protested, but it seemed Matilda's mind was made up, and for once, Eleanor agreed with her.

I left them at the shop after thanking them and drove away, intending to head home. I hadn't gone far when I thought I should take a detour to Sarah Beiler's house and ask her about coolant. After all, it was the last piece of the puzzle. While in the café I had googled it. The website said most coolant varieties did have an added bittering agent, and it didn't make sense to me that Gemma would drink something bitter. Sarah had a wealth of knowledge about all things medical, not just herbs.

When I arrived, there was no sign of anybody, so I walked up the porch and knocked on the door. Sarah opened it. She looked surprised to see me but quickly recovered. "*Wunderbar*! It's *gut* to see you, Jane." "*Wie gehts?*"

"I'm well, thank you."

Sarah ushered me inside. "Come in, come in. This is good timing. I've just made a batch of chocolate whoopie pies with vanilla buttercream, and I've just brewed some meadow tea."

"That sounds good." I followed her into the kitchen. Just as I did, there was a loud clap of thunder directly above us. I jumped. "That came out of nowhere," I said. "I did see the dark clouds gathering, but I could still see blue skies."

Sarah looked out the kitchen window. "The skies won't be blue for long." She crossed to the gas lamp in the middle of the room, opened the wooden cupboard door and turned it on. Light flooded the room. *At least the Amish don't have to worry about thunderstorms causing power outages*, I thought with amusement.

Sarah poured me a cup of tea and urged me to eat some whoopie pies. I didn't need any encouragement. When I had eaten two, she said, "You're here to get my advice about the murder."

I had almost forgotten how quickly news spreads in the Amish community. "That's right," I said. "One thing in particular puzzles me. The poison was ethylene glycol."

"Coolant," she said.

I nodded. "It was found in a hip flask which also contained brandy but appeared to be full. There were also shot glasses lined up in the office the victim had been using. She was a committee member of the goat show."

Sarah nodded. I pushed on. "It was green. Maybe she mistook it for something else. I mean, obviously she did or she wouldn't be dead."

"And what puzzles you?" Sarah asked me.

"The taste," I said. "I've read that ethylene glycol is a sweet tasting liquid and that it can actually taste quite nice. However, I've read that a bittering agent is added to it so people and animals won't drink by mistake and die."

"The bittering agent was only added in recent years, if I understand correctly," Sarah said. "I think it was in 2012, but you had better check."

That surprised me. "So if somebody had a bottle of coolant lying around from before that time, it would taste sweet."

Sarah nodded. "Exactly. Any bottles made prior to that date would taste sweet, and nobody would be any the wiser. If anything, they might simply think their drink was a little sweeter than it should be."

"I haven't been able to find out how much the victim consumed," I said, "but would one shot glass be enough to kill her?"

"How big is a shot glass?" Sarah asked me.

"One and a half fluid ounces, I believe. Actually, I was told that one ounce of ethylene glycol is fatal in humans."

Sarah was eating a chocolate whoopie pie. When she finished it, she said, "Ethylene glycol is actually quite deadly. It only takes a small amount to kill a full-grown human. Even a single mouthful would require hospitalization for the victim."

"Would it take a nurse or somebody with specific medical knowledge to know that?" I asked her.

She laughed. "You're an *Englischer*; you should know that anybody could simply find poisons on the Internet. I'm sure you'll find there have been many several notable poisoning cases where ethylene glycol has been used."

My meadow tea was quite hot. I sipped it gingerly before saying, "Yes, I did find several cases of deliberate poisoning by ethylene glycol. An English woman put antifreeze in her husband's cherry Lambrini—Lambrini is pear cider. He spent several days in a coma and needed rehabilitation for one year. Closer to home, a woman murdered her first husband and then her subsequent husband, by putting antifreeze in their food. I found numerous other cases."

Sarah nodded. "Is there anything else you wanted to know?"

I shook my head. "No. Thanks, Sarah, you've been a big help."

Sarah chuckled. "I don't think I told you anything you didn't already know."

I corrected her. "Actually, you *have* been a big help because you told me the bittering agent was added only in 2012."

"I could be wrong about the precise year," Sarah said. "You had better check it."

I nodded. "Thanks, I will, but it's helpful to know that anybody could have it lying around in their garage. Most people have old products lying around."

"Does that help narrow down your suspects?"

I ran my hand over my eyes. My first instinct was to say, "No," but then I thought on it some more. "Actually, it does help in that I now won't go looking for pharmacists, or people in the medical profession, or people who have special access to laboratories, or other things like that."

Still, while I was trying to put a positive spin on it, I was quite deflated. Anybody at all could have a pre-2012 bottle of antifreeze in their garage. And anybody simply had to google poisons to discover the fatal dose rate and to know that it had been successfully used in murders previously. This wasn't helping me get any closer to the killer.

Another thunderclap sounded, and I jumped again. "Sounds like that storm's getting closer," Sarah said.

I stood up. "Thanks for your help again, Sarah. I'd better get home or I'll get drenched running from the car to the house."

As I drove away, the rain started to ease somewhat. Just as it did so, a bright yellow car passed me. Could it possibly be Horatio's car?

I turned around as soon as I could and drove in that direction. At first, I thought that the car had gotten too far ahead of me, but I soon caught up. I hung back so as not to make him suspicious.

I didn't even know if it was Horatio's car, but right now I was all out of options. I was glad that he kept driving, and half an hour later, I was glad my car was full of gas. I watched as the car turned down a private road in a remote area. I parked under the cover of a black walnut tree and waited until the car was out of sight.

I sat there, debating what to do. It might not have been Horatio's car at all. Still, the road obviously led to private property, and I didn't want to be trapped there, especially if Horatio was the murderer. I knew it wasn't Horatio's official address as one of the first things we did was to search his address online.

I was still pondering what to do when another car came along. It slowed down to take the turn. As it did, so I caught a good look at the driver. It was Cynthia.

Just then, Cynthia turned and looked straight at me.

22

Without thinking, I crouched down in the seat. This, no doubt, looked suspicious, but it was too late. When I looked up again, Cynthia's car was parked at the start of the private driveway, but the rain was coming down too hard to see inside.

I immediately drove away in the opposite direction. Had Cynthia recognized me from the distance? I tried to call Matilda and tell her that there was no cell phone service. I looked in the rearview mirror, but I couldn't see a car following me.

I took a deep breath to calm my nerves. Was Cynthia the woman who was having an affair with Horatio? I remembered something. She had said she was at the show watching the goat classes, but she hadn't seen Gigi eat the judge's beard, and that had been the only class in the ring at the time. Of course, that wasn't exactly incriminating, because she might have been drinking coffee or chatting to somebody and not actually looking in the ring.

What seemed more suspicious was Cynthia's falling out with Gemma which had lasted a few months. Gemma discovered her son's relationship with a woman several months ago. The timing was spot on.

The rain came down harder. I decided to drive straight home and call Damon to tell him what I had discovered. He would be angry with me for following Horatio, but I didn't have an option.

When I got home, I cut the engine, slammed the door, locked it remotely over my shoulder, and sprinted up the stairs into the house. I turned on the light, but just as I did so there was a flash of forked lightning, and the lights went out.

I was soaked right through. I needed to have a nice warm shower, but first, I called Damon. To my dismay, it went straight to voicemail. I stared at the phone in disbelief and then left him a message. I immediately called Matilda. "Don't let Rebecca hear what I'm saying because I don't want to worry her," I said, "but I think Cynthia and Horatio were in it together."

"Yes, do go on," Matilda said in a monotone.

I told Matilda all about it, how I had followed Horatio to a private road and how Cynthia had turned up and had looked at my car. I finished by saying, "I called Damon, but it went straight to voicemail."

"And did you leave a message?"

"Yes, of course I did," I said. "Anyway, she didn't follow me."

"Can you be certain?"

I shook my head but then realized nobody could see me. "No, I can't be certain. It was raining heavily, but I don't think I was followed."

Matilda must have gone outside to speak because I could now hear traffic sounds in the background. She said firmly, "Jane, lock all the doors and don't let anybody in. Be very careful. You said she saw you?"

"She looked straight at the car, but I don't know whether or not she saw me."

"We can't take any chances. Do you have any weapons?"

"Weapons?" I said in disbelief. "Of course not!"

Matilda sighed. "Then keep trying Damon, and Eleanor and I will catch a taxi straight home."

I was about to protest but simply said, "Thanks." I hung up and took the stairs two at a time to the bathroom. I was absolutely drenched and wanted to have a very quick shower. I was halfway up the stairs when the lights came back on. "Thank goodness," I muttered to myself.

After my shower, I quickly threw on some nice clothes and some make-up in case Damon came here when he got my message. I walked down the stairs and into the living room.

To my shock, Mr. Crumbles was sitting in the chandelier. "Mr. Crumbles, get down from there at once!" I scolded him. "How did you get up there?"

Of course, I knew how he had gotten up there. There was a ladder perched directly under the chandelier. Matilda had intended to change out the light globes for energy-efficient ones. Mr. Crumbles had climbed up the ladder, the attraction of the sparkling chandelier tassels obviously too much for him. He was perched there precariously, one paw outstretched and swiping at intervals at the sparkling chandelier tassels.

I walked over to the ladder, intending to climb up, when I suddenly realized that Mr. Crumbles would not come willingly. I walked over to the coffee table to check my phone. I must have been going mad, as I was certain I had left it on the couch right by Eleanor's discarded socks. Still, nobody had called.

"Damon, where are you?" I said to the phone. I left it there and walked into the kitchen to fetch some kitty treats to entice Mr. Crumbles down from the chandelier.

Just as I walked back into the living room, I heard a sound. I walked over to test the front door. Thankfully, it was still locked. I peeked out the window and saw another car. I gasped. That looked like the car I had seen Cynthia driving.

But where was she? My blood ran cold.

I turned around, intending to run for my phone to call 911.

Cynthia was barring my way. She was brandishing a large butcher knife. "How did you know it was me?" she snapped. Gone was her pleasant, socialite demeanor. Her expression was that of a madwoman.

"I, I wasn't certain until now," I sputtered. "How did you get in?"

"One of the windows wasn't locked." She spoke fast.

"Oh well, I've already called the police, and they're on their way here now."

"You've made two calls, one to somebody called Damon and one to that old woman,

Matilda," she said smugly. "I looked through your phone while you were upstairs."

"Damon is a homicide detective," I told her. "His name is Detective Damon McCloud."

She sneered at me. "How gullible do you think I am?"

I sized up the distance between us. She could close the ground to me fairly quickly. She had a large knife, and I did not.

Matilda and Eleanor were on their way, so I had to stall for time. "So, let me get this straight," I said. "You had a bottle of coolant from before 2012 that didn't have the bittering agent in it."

"Yes, I did," she said. "And it smelled delicious too."

"And you poured it into a shot glass and gave it to Gemma to drink."

"She drank it without batting an eyelid," Cynthia said in boastful tones. "It was quite a pleasant shade of green."

"So what did she think it actually was?" I asked.

Gemma's expression darkened. "How should I know? I told her it was absinthe. I assume she believed me."

"But didn't you and Gemma have a falling out when she found out you and Horatio were still dating?"

Cynthia let out a string of obscenities. "She couldn't mind her own business! Yes, she threatened to cut him out of the will. He had to pretend we weren't dating for a long time. Somehow, she found out we were, so she said she was cutting Horatio out of the will. She even made an appointment with her lawyer. That's when we knew we had to kill her before she actually did change her will."

One thing puzzled me. "Then how did you get her to drink the shot? I mean, she was angry with you, so why would she drink shots with you?"

Cynthia smirked at me. "Because I did a rather good acting job, if I do say so myself. I told her that I was in love with Horatio, but that she had won. I said I couldn't live with myself if she cut Horatio out of the will and she believed me. I told her I was leaving for California and I was going to live there with my sister and start a new life. I begged her not to tell Horatio and said I would tell him."

"And she believed that?"

Cynthia smirked at me. "Not at first, but yes, she did. Anyway, enough talking."

"This is your last chance," I said. "Give yourself up or it will be the worse for you."

She looked at me as though I had taken leave of my senses. "Are you stark raving mad? I have this." She waved the huge knife at me. "And you don't have a weapon."

"Oh yes, I do," I said. "I have these." I waved the packet of cat treats at her. They were Mr. Crumbles' favorite treats, little bits of tuna, dry inside but moist on the outside.

She broke into raucous laughter. "You *have* gone mad. That's not a weapon."

"Don't say I didn't warn you." I tipped the contents into my hand and threw them at her. She was still laughing as they hit her and landed her hair.

The next thing I knew, Mr. Crumbles leaped from the chandelier onto her head to eat the treats. Cynthia screamed with fright and dropped the knife. As she frantically moved around, trying to dislodge him, Mr. Crumbles dug his claws into her head to keep his balance. Cynthia spun in circles, screaming obscenities at the top of her lungs with Mr.

Crumbles digging his claws in harder and harder.

I ran over to her and kicked the knife away, just as Matilda and Eleanor burst through the door. It all happened so quickly, I could scarcely believe my eyes.

Eleanor grabbed Mr. Crumbles in one move. I could hear him purring loudly even over Cynthia's screams. Clearly, he had been enjoying himself.

At the same time, Matilda did what looked to me to be jujitsu moves on Cynthia and pinned her to the ground. "Rope!" she called out.

I hadn't even seen Eleanor leave the room, but there she was suddenly by Matilda's side with a length of rope. Matilda hogtied Cynthia, before grabbing Eleanor's sock from the couch and shoving it in a protesting Cynthia's mouth. Mr. Crumbles was still purring loudly.

Matilda turned to me. "I can hear sirens. Get your story ready, Jane. You will need to tell the police that you were the one who tied up Cynthia. You have to leave me out of it."

23

I had known the Pet Protection classes would change Mr. Crumbles. I simply had not anticipated how much.

Mr. Crumbles no longer looked like Mr. Crumbles. Mr. Crumbles is now looked like a cat cop. He wore tiny aviators, and a navy jacket that read *FBI*.

My mouth dropped open. "Eleanor, our cat does not work for the Federal Bureau of Investigation."

"No," Eleanor said, cutting an elegant figure as she bobbled out of the footpath in five-inch heels. "FBI stands for the Feline Bureau of Investigation."

My face burned. "Take that jacket off him before Damon sees him," I pleaded. I tugged at my collar, letting cool air tickle my throat. It was bad enough that Eleanor had enrolled Mr. Crumbles in Pet Protection classes—I didn't need Damon to see the complete and utter madness that ran in my household.

Matilda squealed as she stepped from the house. "Oh look! Mr. Crumbles is ready to catch some purr-petrators."

I looked at Matilda, shocked. "Matilda, please don't tell me you of all people are enjoying this."

"Jane, look at that tiny little jacket. He's so cute!"

Eleanor beamed. "Aaron spoke with conviction when he said Mr. Crumbles has the most powerful toes he'd ever seen."

"More like spoke with *confection* as Aaron was eating one of Rebecca's cupcakes at the time," Matilda said. "Still, I always knew that cat would make something of himself. He solved that murder all on his own."

"He didn't solve the murder," I said in exasperation. "I had already figured out that Cynthia was the murderer and in it with Horatio."

"Mr. Crumbles must have overheard what I said about cats jumping on enemies' heads when they were storming a fortress," Matilda said smugly. "He used the same technique on Cynthia. I knew it would work!"

Eleanor rubbed Mr. Crumbles behind the ear. "Mr. Crumbles needs to be a detective. Then murderers wouldn't even think of murdering. They know a cat was on the case."

"Who is on the case?"

I jumped as Damon closed his car door. I hadn't even noticed him arrive. "Nothing. No one. Matilda and Eleanor were just taking Mr. Crumbles inside." I stepped in front of the cat hoping that Damon had not seen the FBI jacket.

"Damon, your girlfriend is being very unsupportive," Matilda said.

"Matilda!" I sputtered.

Damon's face turned bright red.

I bent over and scooped Mr. Crumbles into my arms. There was no point in trying to hide his outfit anymore. "I'm sorry, Damon. Matilda and Eleanor have been taken over by body snatchers. As you know, Eleanor enrolled Mr. Crumbles in Pet Protection classes."

"His toes are very powerful," Eleanor confirmed.

"I can see that." Damon tickled Mr. Crumbles under the chin. "Good boy."

"Put him down, Jane. He is clearly interested in following a clue." Eleanor snatched Mr. Crumbles out of my arms and placed him on the ground. He at once shot off into the bushes.

"He's not a detective, Eleanor." I brushed a loose strand of hair out of my eyes. The whole world had clearly gone mad. "He saw a mouse or something."

"A criminal mouse."

I sighed. "No, just a regular mouse."

"If it's just a regular mouse, then why is Mr. Crumbles chasing it?"

I slammed the palm of my hand against my head. "Because Mr. Crumbles is a cat!"

Damon interrupted us. "Jane, could I maybe have a word?"

I nodded and followed Damon as he walked toward his car. I pretended not to notice that Matilda was pulling faces behind my back.

"Who knew so much drama could happen around goats?" Damon said with a chuckle as he leaned against his car. He looked very handsome, dressed in a white cable knit sweater, jeans, and a pair of dark blue Chukkas. "So, what's new with you?"

"Nothing." I folded my arms. I was determined not to look over my shoulder at Matilda and Eleanor, who were now crouched on all fours accidentally flashing their underwear to the entire world as they called encouragement to Mr. Crumbles who was now hiding beneath the house.

Damon cleared his throat. "Do you like dinner?"

"Dinner? Yes, I like dinner."

Damon chuckled. "I mean, would you like to have dinner with me? One where I don't have to run out on a case? Not that I can promise that," he added lamely, "but I'll have one of the other detectives cover for me."

"When, now?"

"Oh so, so you are using me to escape from Matilda and Eleanor? I see how it is. I bring you flowers and I ask you out on a romantic date and you only say yes to get away from your housemates."

My heart beat out of my chest. "You didn't bring me flowers," was all I could say.

"Didn't I now?" Damon opened his passenger door and picked up a bouquet of beautiful red roses. "These are for you."

"Thank you." I trembled. I couldn't think of anything else to say.

"So, yes? To dinner?"

I smiled at him. He was standing close. "I already said yes."

Damon smiled. "Yes in the sense of you really truly want to let me take you to dinner? Not yes in the sense that you really truly need to escape from your FBI cat?"

I chuckled then. "There is no escaping my FBI cat. He's ruthless. He has the most powerful toes in all of America."

"So I've heard."

Inside the restaurant was warm with soft, romantic lighting. Damon placed his hand on the small of my back and guided me to our table, which was tucked in the corner beneath a beautiful candelabra. I was grateful for the candlelight. I wasn't much good at applying make-up, and any type of harsh lighting would no doubt make that apparently clear.

Dinner, this time, went by without a hitch. Damon was charming and I found myself light-hearted and giggly. Damon even ordered me another slice of cake for dessert.

I left the restaurant feeling pleasantly happy delighted.

On the way home, we sang along to a cheesy song on the radio. I knew how the world looked at a woman my age—or to be more precise, *didn't* look at a woman my age. The world expected dashing detectives like Damon McCloud to chase younger women, but here he was, driving me home, not worried in the least about my wrinkles or my not-perfectly-flat stomach. I stepped from his car giddily and walked with him to my door.

Damon followed, slightly unsteady on his feet. That perplexed me a little as he had not ordered alcohol with dinner.

"Are you okay?" I asked quietly, not wanting Matilda and Eleanor to burst from the house and ruin the moment as they usually did.

"You make me dizzy," he replied.

I felt my heart stop. Damon stepped forward and took me into his arms. He smelled warm and masculine, with a hint of some familiar, nostalgic spice, like cinnamon. Or maybe cloves. I didn't feel in control of my senses anymore. I felt like a flustered schoolgirl.

"May I kiss you?" Damon asked.

"Detective, I thought you would never ask."

And so I stood in Damon McCloud's arms, kissing him as though we were in Paris, France, beneath the twinkling lights of the Eiffel Tower. Of course, we were actually in Lancaster, Pennsylvania—but if Matilda or Eleanor had told this to either of us, we would never have believed them. Not right now. Not as we stood there in each other's arms, home at last.

AMISH RECIPE

Amish Funny Cake Pie

The chocolate layer sinks to the bottom, hence the name, *Cake Pie*—it's a combination cake + pie!

1 unbaked 9 inch pie shell

Cake Layer (Top Part)

1 cup granulated sugar
1 beaten egg
1/4 cup cold salted butter
1 cup all-purpose flour
1/2 cup milk
1 teaspoon baking powder
1/2 teaspoon vanilla

Preheat oven to 350 degrees.
Cream butter and sugar.
Whisk egg and milk.
Mix flour and baking powder.
Add the combined egg and milk alternately
with flour and baking powder.
Stir in vanilla.
Set aside until Chocolate Layer is prepared.

Chocolate Layer (Lower Part)

1/2 cup granulated sugar
6 tablespoons water
4 tablespoons cocoa
1/4 teaspoon vanilla

Combine sugar, water, cocoa, and vanilla.
Pour into the unbaked pie shell. Pour the
cake later over the top.
Bake for 35 - 40 minutes.
Cool pie on wire pack.
Enjoy!

AMISH RECIPE

Amish Bible Cake

The Amish Bible Cake is also known as *Old Testament Cake* and *Scripture Cake*, as every ingredient is said to be mentioned in the Old Testament.

The ingredients and Scriptures attached to each ingredient do vary between Plain communities and have varied over time.

1/2 cup water *Genesis 24:11*
1/2 cup almonds *Genesis 43:11*
2 teaspoons baking powder *Exodus 12:15*
Cinnamon *Exodus 30:23*
Spices *1 King 10:10*
1/2 teaspoon salt *Leviticus 2:13*
1/2 cup butter *Judges 5:25*
1 cup figs *I Samuel 30:12*
1 cup raisins *I Samuel 30:12*
2 cups flour *I Kings 4:22*
3 large eggs *Isaiah 10:14*
1 1/2 cups sugar *Jeremiah 6:20*
1 tablespoon honey *Proverbs 24:13*
3 tablespoons milk *Judges 4:19*

Preheat oven to 375 degrees.
Butter and flour a cake pan.
Cream butter and sugar.
Add spices and salt.

Separate egg yolks from whites.

Beat egg yolks and add to the mixture.

Sift baking powder with flour and fold in.

Add water and honey.

Place fruit and nuts in a food blender to break down well, then fold into the mixture.

Fold in stiffly beaten egg whites.

Pour into cake pan and sprinkle sugar on top.

Bake for 60 minutes.

NEXT BOOK IN THIS SERIES
AN AMISH CUPCAKE COZY MYSTERY
BOOK 5

An Instant Confection

Jane Delight is looking for a fresh start, and believes her new home will dough the trick. But as a batter of fact, her mischievous cat, Mr. Crumbles, has found a body beneath the floorboards in the bread of night!

Jane's eccentric housemates, octogenarians Matilda and Eleanor, are all done and crusted with mayhem, but will stop at nothing to help Jane. Joining the trio is dishy detective

Damon McCloud, who is determined to see that the murderer gets his just desserts before he can make a bake for it.

ABOUT RUTH HARTZLER

USA Today best-selling author Ruth Hartzler spends her days writing, walking her dog, and thinking of ways to murder somebody. That's because Ruth writes mysteries and thrillers.

She is best known for her archeological adventures, for which she relies upon her former career as a college professor of ancient languages and Biblical history.

www.ruthhartzler.com

Made in the USA
Coppell, TX
01 May 2021

54830276R00194